About the Author

John Whittaker grew up in a small village in the Pennine hills of East Lancashire.

His career led him to live in Durham, Oxford and Lancaster with short spells in Canada. It hardly, he thinks, prepared him to write fiction.

These years were spent with his late wife and their two sons.

With retirement close to the English Lake District more time was released for walking hills and mountains often with friends and family.

Now married to a musician with two sons, there are four grandchildren to watch growing up.

NO PIC-NIC IN CUMBRIA

John Whittaker

NO PIC-NIC IN CUMBRIA

Olympia Publishers
London

www.olympiapublishers.com
OLYMPIA PAPERBACK EDITION

A CIP catalogue record for this title is
available from the British Library.

ISBN: 978-1-80074-301-4

Some references to historical events, real people, or real places are
used fictitiously. Other names, characters, places and events are
products of the author's imagination and any resemblance to actual
events, places or persons, living or dead is entirely coincidental.

First Published in 2022

Olympia Publishers
Tallis House
2 Tallis Street
London
EC4Y 0AB
Printed in Great Britain

Acknowledgements

Some of the characters from the past are real people of the period, but the storyline is just that, a story. For many of the facts, however, particularly of Turner's journey I have relied a great deal on David Hill's excellent account of it, for which I am extremely grateful. In fact it sowed in my mind the idea for the plot.

Most other persona, with the main exceptions of those of the Lancaster Gillow company and Lady Ann Clifford of Appleby, are fictitious, especially those introduced in Parts II and VI.

Whether writing fact or fiction, I take full responsibility for wild imaginings or downright errors.

The descriptions and timings of Part VI rely a good deal on a day's exploration of the terrain and geography conducted on foot in the company of my son Roger and grandson Fergus when the latter was ten years of age. He is a first-rate yomper. Our expedition was from Dufton via Rundale, High Cup Nick and Hannah's Well, then back to the Stag Inn.

My hours at the laptop allowed Wendy to spend time with her beloved violin, a background sound whose beauty provided calm for me at times when the writing and typing did not.

PART 1

To travel hopefully is a better thing than to arrive, and the true success is to labour
R L Stevenson

CHAPTER 1

It is 1816. The year of no summer.

"This is where we part, William, until you return to us."

The little party had reached a milestone near the picturesque village of Malham in the Yorkshire Dales as they returned home to Otley. Mr Fawkes had caused Jenks his coachman to stop the horses. William and the Fawkes family had together been enjoying a peaceful few days with Fawkes's friends at Browsholme Hall. William had been planning his expedition there with the help of maps in the library which showed the more important tracks and bridleways.

But he was an active man to whom rest was time wasted.

The fine coach and four horses had brought them to their parting for William was anxious to begin his explorations to the north. Their passage through farmlands and villages had been noted by labourers in the fields who seldom saw such grandeur and style at which to jab fingers and provide chit-chat to lighten a grinding day.

Not for decades had the skies been so forbidding and the crops so sparse.

***

Jenks the postillion brought William's horse up to the coach from its position behind. Hector was as ready as his master to go unimpeded on bridle paths and away from the stony and sometimes muddy stretches of road which gave service to wheels as well as hooves.

"I'm obliged to you Jenks. Put that package carefully in Hector's saddlebags and saddle me up for a rough ride. I thank you kindly, Mr Fawkes and now I must take my leave. You can be sure I will look after Hector and bring him safely back to your stables, but it is more a question of him looking after me."

A cockney accent stood out in West Yorkshire like a Welshman in Patagonia.

"You will come back to us, William, when your travels are over. We must see the fruits of your labours." But he knew that only early signs would be visible then and the fully formed items might not be seen for months or even years.

"Take care. There is wild country ahead of you with even wilder weather."

"We will miss William you know until he returns," said Fawkes to his children, "even if he doesn't miss us. You will most miss him for I know you like his company when he has time to play, especially you young Hawksworth, or Hawkey as he likes to say. But you will all remember his kindly help with your art work and especially the birds you did together," Walter said this and admitted that his friend's time with the children was quite unexpected for such a withdrawn and busy man.

"At least he looked happy in anticipating a trek which will surely take him four weeks if he goes hell for leather. I pity that horse we sent him off on, but Hector is as good as they come for a ride over the rough. Come children we must return to Farnley."

The children were excited by the pitching and tossing of their stately vehicle as its huge wheels ground their way over the rough road. Some of the jarring was eased by the enormous leaf springs suspending their cabin above the bouncing axles. They loved to peep out around the gorgeous draperies at the windows and even stare at the workers in the fields.

"Don't poke fun at those fine men and women," insisted Mrs Fawkes. "They provide our daily bread and meat and this year is not good for farming." Her sternness soon gave way to a smile whilst she thought of entertaining their young family.

"Our journey will be more than one hour, children. Shall we see if your domino game can be played on this board over my knees?" The boys liked to see the bones topple which indeed they soon did with the swaying of the coach, but they were learning to deal with the numbers and how to play their new game.

"I love the patterns you make with the tiles as they creep across the board."

***

Now on much rougher terrain, their recent companions, man and horse, allowed little conversation to interrupt their thoughts between the moments when they had to communicate to cross exceptionally rough parts. The rider felt that he knew more of the mind of his steed than that of even his nearest and dearest. But Hector kept his eyes and hooves firmly on the track whilst his master allowed his eyes and imagination to roam all over the landscape. At least the saddlebags were light on Hector's back for his master travelled with little more than the tools of his trade and a change of clothes, and the horse could be comforted by the appearance of a nosebag from their mysterious depths. William cared little for the outward signs of his position in society and could even have been called careless in dress and manner.

He was putting his conventional life on hold and allowing himself the utter joy of being without the need for people-conversation, though Mr Fawkes was a man he had come to admire and they were close to becoming friends. But he didn't want or need the company of men when so much was to be gained by contemplation of all around him. It mattered not to him whether the sun shone or the rains poured. This was wilder and yet wilder nature which thrust its character on him ever more in wind and rain than in more tranquil moments. Sometimes as clouds dispersed, the vistas were immense and dominance of foreground colour gave way to distant blues and purples.

The hours passed as if moments whilst meadows with their swathes of floral colour, and hillsides with peacefully grazing sheep were replaced by brown moorland, rock outcrops and crashing watercourses. The sheep were quite unlike those in the countryside he had passed much nearer to the start of what was to become an epic journey. Here they were stockier and greyer, tougher and more resilient as they needed to be in these valleys and hills of Swaledale, Wensleydale and Teesdale. They, like their observer, needed little time with men for they were as much a part of the land as he hoped to be in his bid to *feel* his surroundings as much as see them.

***

It seemed long ago since he had asked his boy Simon to pack his bags as frugally as possible with the coach to Grantham leaving in two hours.

"I'll be glad to leave London again," he had said. "Don't forget my country clothes and my equipment though I shall need to dress more correctly staying in Yorkshire with my patrons."

As before, he had been kindly received in the Fawkes household and allowed, nay encouraged to pursue his work there with the utmost vigour. He liked to make time for the children, especially young Hawkey who loved to be chased around the orchard and pushed on a makeshift swing hanging from a tree. The girls enjoyed their lessons more when he was there to help and tell them stories of his life in London, so far away. The Fawkes family did have their house in London, but the journey was so rough and the children were rarely there.

In time Mr Fawkes had needed to visit his friends at Browsholme and his route provided his London visitor with a start to his private expedition. A luxury start indeed to a month when comfort was to be denied and even life itself to be nearly threatened. A whole month on horseback lay ahead for William.

***

The first part of his journey passed through countryside which he had seen before and did not delay him too much. So far, the inns like the Morritt Arms at Rokeby had been comfortable and welcoming and the roads were kind to man and horse.

"We are going to have to cover some ground today Hector. We are heading for spectacular dales and hills with many of the most exciting vistas in England for us to see and note. You must have lots of water and good grain for our journey together. The stone troughs along the bridleways will give you good drinking and we can buy grain at the farms as we go. We shall seek night's rest at Middleton or perhaps Langdon Beck where you will have warm stabling."

Next morning they were confronted by one of the finest river sights in England.

"Look, Hector at the way the brown water loaded with peat cascades over the rocky rim to crash into the pool more than fifty feet below and to cut back a gorge the sight of which has made travellers tremble since first they trod these parts, and named it High Force. Can you imagine, Hector how this wonder thrills the mind of the son of a poor hairdresser from London? If you have struggled to get me here beyond Low Force, remember our more restful times in beautiful Richmond and worldly Middleton. This is a ravine we can't get over and we must seek our way west by crossing upstream. More rain and I shall be as web-footed as a drake."

They tracked north past Falcon Clints and found another great obstacle, Cauldron Snout. Whoever coined these names had a way with words but needed little imagination to see a home for raptors and a veritable seething of waters as they fall some 200 feet over a distance of 150 yards.

In all Hector and his master had climbed 300 feet in the last four miles and criss-crossed this plummeting mighty river at three points. Few rivers can gather so much water in so short a distance from its source below the plateau of Cross Fell, the highest summit in the whole Pennine range. Man and horse were soon to understand why in their next and last adventure over the worst terrain in this epic trek as they sought to reach Appleby to the south and west.

They had reached their farthest point north, but not the highest. That was still to come, but not with ease. The ride from Cauldron Snout took Hector across the highest, roughest, toughest and in parts boggiest stretch of the whole journey. At first some signs of a track, but soon giving way on days as wet as this to little short of a quagmire or moss where even strong horses could founder in the waterlogged peat. Here was a source of the brown water they had seen cascading down the Cauldron and High Force. Even bedrock was sometimes revealed in the washed-out gulleys between raised hags and occasionally were uncovered traces of the blackened timbers of birch from some 3000 years ago, and fragments of *Bos* cattle which once roamed these fells. These sights, even to our exceptionally observant traveller were lost today in the need for horse and rider to battle heads down against the storm. Gallant Hector had struggled, sometimes with bog above his hocks and mud caked up his flanks. Even the driving rain failed to wash mud from horse and rider though the latter cared less about himself than about his steed and especially the need to protect valuable contents of panniers from drenching. Perhaps any horseman would wish to keep meagre possessions dry but, to this rider, they were his livelihood and products of his boundless creativity finding expression many times at every stage of this epic journey. The blanket bogs, the sphagnum moss; traps for unwary horses and exhausted men beckoned them on as a siren lures travellers to possible doom. Perhaps that would have been his fate and even Hector's if a figure had not appeared to them through the swirling mists and penetrating rain. Was it man or spectre? Who would be active in these wastes on such a day as this? With the Swaledale sheep still on the fells for which they were hefted, their shepherd had braved these heights to check his toughened charges. Turning their grizzled faces away from the biting wind, the animals lined up to see him with his countenance reddened and coarsened from a lifetime with them on these hills. But for a moment his shepherding instincts were suspended by glimpses of man and horse sometimes emerging from, and then to be swallowed up by, the swirling mist and drenching rain.

"Where are you bound, sir?" he shouted against the blasting wind known as the Helm in these parts.

"We are for Appleby," replied the weary traveller on his near exhausted, mud-soaked mount.

"Well you're past the worst, sir. There is them oo'd stay in shelter on such a day. But them such as thee willn' make Appleby afore sunset. T' Buck a' Dufton is place for thee and 'im. Tek a rest for t'orse oer yon crest. 'tis 'igh cup nick and not a bigger cleft to be seen in these parts, nor 'tis sed for many a score o' miles. We'ther be liftin' and sheep be raising yeds agin. Dufton be four miles beyond on yezzy ground. Th'l do 'e well at Buck on't village green."

A sodden, mud-spattered and exhausted rider could at that moment only think 'what a confounded fag' this part of the journey had been. He had taken four hours to cover eleven miles despite Hector's strength. Now that the storm had abated somewhat and clouds lifted a little, they soon arrived at the place known to the locals as High Cup Nick. On their right were nodding white heads of an expanse of cotton grasses indicating wet ground unsuitable for Hector. Immediately beneath his feet to the south was the grandest sight in the whole of the Pennine chain. Its name might suggest little more than a notch in the valley crest, but the valley below stretched out for hundreds of feet with a prominent truly vertical upper lip of Whin Sill dolerite itself near eighty feet high but hanging over the valley base hundreds of feet below. Such a barrier of intruded volcanic rock had formed High Force and Cauldron Snout seen earlier that day but now ten miles behind, and unknown to him even farther away at Crag Lough on Hadrian's Wall and at Bamburgh Castle rock.

***

With a sharp intake of breath the rider saw the High Cup as the subject of what he, more than any other man of his time in all England, could capture with deft strokes of his hand. For our traveller is Master Turner given the names Joseph Mallord William by his mother and barber father who brought him up in poverty in London.

"We will call him William after me," said his father. He found no objection from his wife who sadly was now losing her mind. Although his father had done his utmost to support young William and to encourage him in his art, London held no special delights for the young man and he felt released on his returns to his friends and his travels in the North.

That son was already famous, even a household name, at least in those rich houses privileged to buy his incomparable paintings. These often began as quick, almost cursory sketches sometimes on rather scrappy detached sheets or in sketchbooks for more important subjects, usually those commissioned by publishers like Longman of travel books of the age. The suited and cravatted men at Longmans could not have known how much their client had braved, together with his trusty companion and transport, to reach many of the remote commissioned vistas. No part more so than the ride from the roaring waters of the Tees to this dry valley carved out into a great U-shape by a massive glacier but protected at its rims by the hard rock of the Whin Sill. Turner looked down to an amphitheatre cut into the south-facing flanks of a ridge of hills soon to form to the north west of him the barriers of Great and Little Dun Fells and the mighty Cross Fell, the highest point in the Pennine range. Behind them and out of sight to our travellers rises the Tees flowing within 200 yards of the source of another mighty river, the South Tyne. But the plunging Tees is destined to reach the sea at Middlesbrough thirty miles from its brother flowing rather more sedately to the north at Newcastle.

Not deterred by the elements around him, Turner dismounted and struggled to hold against the wind his smallest sketchbooks. An observer might have seen him make only a few deft pencil strokes executed quickly whilst Hector, temporarily relieved of his burden attempted to benefit from seeking out food amongst predominantly inedible silicon-loaded Nardus grass. But to his master, the contrasting greens and browns (mostly the latter) of this upland vegetation against which was set the grey/brown of the ravine's rim, constituted a scene which he would commit so precisely to memory that only a black and white sketch was needed to retain it. The image could be transformed in a bare and untidy studio in London to turn thoughts and feelings into a masterpiece which would endure for centuries and become as sought after as any in the English style. The sketch completed, William now thought of the Fawkes family to which he would return bearing many such drafts, a number of which when completed they might add to those on their walls at Farnley to make a collection of which he, as well as his sponsors could feel justly proud. They knew, as much as he did, that no person would ever match them. He could not yet anticipate that within his lifetime they were to become so sought after that fifty guineas would reach his bank. He would become a rich man. For now, his urge was simply to capture these sights, not just as representative of a scene, but to incorporate his very feelings and deep understandings of what he saw and experienced at each location. Who else would linger in these appalling conditions in order to absorb them as an equal, or even dominant, part of the scene?

CHAPTER 2

Now it was downhill all the way on a good miners' track to Dufton and great comfort at The Buck Inn facing the village green.

William was a very experienced rider and would not seek his own comfort until his horse was looked after. Both of them were drenched. When sweat and mud were removed, unsaddling and rubbing down was expertly done by the inn's ostler and then Hector could be walked around to cool off and be fed and watered after shoes had been inspected for stones.

After seeing to Hector and getting dry and decent in front of a roaring fire, thoughts of the perils of the day melted into satisfaction at the work achieved and the prospects ahead. Such travel might have defeated many a city man but Turner didn't at all mind discomfort – indeed he was rather noted for his somewhat scruffy appearance even when in London. Most important to him now was the gentle drying of wet sketches, including two of High Cup Nick; one showing the very distant prospect of the Lakeland mountains. They were wet with the storms of the journey, not with paint, for he sketched only in pencil and stored colour and atmosphere in his mind for future completion. To someone so enthralled by the wildness of these northern hills of England and so energetic at capturing their character, no time could be better spent and no thoughts more creative. A lesser man would have reflected on the discomforts of the day or even tried to drive them from memory. Genius meant re-living them until they were so much a part of this man that rain and even wind could be ingrained into his art as a permanent record of the event as well as the vast scene. To the man himself, however, genius, in the words of William Hogarth 'is nothing but labour and diligence.'

Even though a short man, Turner was impressed by the low oak beams giving the room a character different from his own home in London which he had designed himself to give light and space, and from his usual experience of inns on his travels. His host was already beckoning him to the fireside and preparing meat and ale to restore him whilst his outer clothing was dried.

"Thank ye Mr Landlord. I have been much comforted and rested in your inn. These parts are special to me and I shall return, hoping to sojourn again by your excellent fireside and take of your ale and lamb's meat."

Our traveller was much impressed by the contrasts between red sandstone buildings, limestone walls and even granite in places. The complex geology gave livelihoods, though very hard, to miners of lead. He had been told by the landlord that important visitors from the London Lead Company came to stay and gave him and his family a good income.

Refreshed and victualled, man and horse crossed the village green, passed the old Dufton Hall and made the eight miles fly by to Appleby town in the county of Westmorland. August was too late in the year to see the historic horse fair with its scores of canvas-topped caravans converging on the town from all over, and horses ridden bareback to be washed in the river prior to being offered for sale to other travellers. Even the townsfolk could hardly have imagined descendants of those travellers filling the town at the fair 200 years after Turner passed by.

Here there were more sketches to be made to give homage to the fine main thoroughfare stretching up from the ancient church with its pillared and recently built portico by Smirke. Turner took a special interest in architecture and applauded this screen providing frontage to the church even though it still looked very new and unweathered. Now he would ride past fine houses of the gentry, alms cottages on the left, to the splendour of the castle overlooking all. In few towns would alms be offered so close to the seat of the ruling family when even the gentry were ensconced below.

In fact, the Earl of Thanet was at home in the castle. It was now largely used only as his country seat and in any case he spent most of his time in France now that he had an illegitimate son there. His family had inherited the property from the descendants of Anne Clifford who herself was the ninth generation of Cliffords to own it since it had passed to them from the Viponts in the thirteenth century. The castle had never been so much alive as it was when she visited on her frequent progressions from Skipton through Mallerstang to her other properties at Pendragon, Brougham and Brough. These last two had even supplied stone for the Thanets' extensions in the late seventeenth century.

"Mr Turner, sir," came an interruption. "My lord at the castle has heard you are in town and would talk with you. Will you walk with me, sir to the castle where your horse will be attended to?"

Overlooking the courtyard of this seat of the Thanet family is Caesar's Tower. Standing at its base was the lord of the house.

"Mr Turner, the message came that you are in town. I am not much now in this house for I reside mostly in Kent and France. But I have seen your paintings at the house of Fawkes on my visits to Otley, and at Harewood. Are you here to paint? I shall be very pleased to see your work and if it be possible to place a picture in my house."

If Lord Thanet expected deference from Turner, he did not receive it.

"My lord, my paintings at this time are commissioned by others and are to illustrate Dr Whitaker's great new work on Yorkshire. First I shall explore to the west into Lancashire before returning across Morecambe Bay to Lancaster and return to Yorkshire. Then to London with my sketchbooks to complete them to send to my engravers and publishers. Indeed they are indebted to me to 3,000 guineas for my work, so nothing must distract me, though I know I shall now be paid in pounds after the guinea was withdrawn last year. But since leaving Yorkshire I have also made some small drawings which might adorn your house one day. Yesterday I was in the rain and wind on the moor above High Cup. Those works will not allow engraving, for it will be more of storm than of scene, and engravers, even the most respected, cannot do justice to my storms."

"Let me show you, Mr Turner, the vista from my keep tower if you will please to climb 100 steps? Since my ancestors caused the tower to be higher than for its 600 years before, across the town, across the dale you can nearly see the Cup of which you speak. It is my joy many a day to climb the steps to come to look at those hills from there. I will gladly make purchase of representation of such a scene especially in those features I shall never myself see, for my carriage cannot reach it. Will you take a pipe with me, sir before you go?"

"I will take a pinch of snuff," said Turner, "and I shall need to restore my stock when I get to Kendal. I hear tell of a wonderful maker named Harrison at Meal Bank on the river Mint."

"Come then into my house," said Thanet as he led the travel-stained figure of the artist through into the panelled entrance hall with its coved ceiling above two storeys, and into his study room off the library. A convivial hour was more than enough for Turner, not a very sociable man, and these grand surroundings had less attraction to him than the delights of his country journey.

"I shall need my horse forthwith," said Turner, "for I have much riding to do today. Good day to you, My lord. I hear your wishes for a painting and will endeavour to comply when all else is done. You must apply to my studio in Harley Street and my agent Griffin."

CHAPTER 3

With these words the tour resumed towards Kendal where snuff would be purchased. Then to the southern Lake District and amazingly, but not unusually at the time, across Morecambe Bay by coach and the relative comfort of the Sun Inn at Lancaster.

The road from Furness Abbey on the north-west side of the bay was conveniently, but dangerously set across the estuaries and expanses of the bay, for this removed nearly twenty miles from the land-based route which was beset by marshes and even brigands in places. The direct route of about eight miles across mudflats had the great advantage of linking both parts of the old Lancashire county but meant crossing ever changing river channels and occasional but very dangerous quicksands. The King's guides since 1548 had endeavoured to ensure safe passage.

"Take care, Hector, men and even horses are sometimes lost in these sands. We must follow our guide and keep close to the coach and other horsemen. I do not wish to be retrieved and interred at Cartmel Priory where they tell me some of those drowned lie."

For Turner an adventure like this was meat and bread and the coach arriving at landfall near Hest Bank hostelry gave opportunity for a sketch, depicting his travails of the crossing in a rainstorm on horseback alongside the crowded Lancaster coach and fellow riders. They had to beat the incoming tide as it raced across the mud flats to fill 120 square miles of the second largest bay in England. In the channel of the river Kent, the rushing water could form a fast moving bore.

"Mr Landlord," said Turner at the Sun Inn, "I hear in London of Mr Richard Gillow of Lancaster, making the finest furniture of the day. Can you say how I might see his work?"

"Yes sir, you need only walk fifty paces across the road toward the castle and you will see his old workshop on the left. He has been much engaged in building a new and larger shop nearer the river, but is often still to be seen in his offices by the castle warden's large house, though his personal interest in the company has begun to decline. Below to the right you will see the sailing ships which bring timber from the Caribbean to Lancaster, and carry back to the merchants' houses there the furniture made to order if it isn't going to the grandest houses in England or Scotland or across wide oceans. When slowly dried that wood is the best that can be found anywhere."

***

A few hours of relaxation were possible as Turner visited the Gillow workshops of which he had heard through his London clients. They sang the praises of these wonderful northern craftsmen and designers whose sought-after products were selling well at the firm's Oxford Street shop to add to lucrative exports around the world. What could provide a more elegant furnishing for their grand London houses than a Gillow library with Turner paintings on the walls? Many with properties designed by John Nash may have had recommendation from him as he wrote at his own beautiful Carlton House desk by Gillow. From now, Turner would himself sing the praises of this enterprise as an artist who did not fail to appreciate other men's artistry and skill.

"Sir, you must meet one of my most trusted craftsmen, William Naylor, to watch his skill and trustworthiness for he has been with us these past thirty years."

Naylor was pleased to talk to another craftsman, even if of a different kind.

"Tell me what you make at your bench, Master Naylor?" enquired the artist.

"Today, sir, I work on a cheveret but I can do much more. I learned my skills over many years. Sometimes I made writing boxes for the gentry travelling from Lancaster to the Americas and for the captains of their ships. They returned with timbers the like of which you have never seen, sir."

Turner watched this man show pride in his work by writing his name, for he could make his mark, by pencil on a drawer liner.

Lancaster offered splendid views of city and across the bay to the Lakeland fells, and the chance to telegraph agent Thomas Griffin to let him know that the tour was going well enough to satisfy his publishers. The city was by now established on the newly emerging tourist routes and chance of a few paintings was not to be missed by Turner with an eye to revenue. There was no court in session so it also offered the opportunity to visit the castle keeper's house below the castle. Here was to be seen how comfortably the visiting judges were accommodated in the splendour of rooms recently furnished in the style of the new Regency century by Gillow. These pieces were in the more restrained designs favoured in the North than the more flamboyant which had became popular in the South following the Regent's own questionable tastes. It was no accident that the North had given birth to England's and Europe's most appreciated furniture designers Chippendale and later Sheraton even if they had to both seek their fortunes, the latter rather unsuccessfully, in London.

***

Progress up the valley of the River Lune was interrupted by sketching and did not allow salmon fishing to satisfy Turner's only real relaxation after his love of music and opera.

"Fishing must wait, Hector, till we return to Farnley and Fawkes provides rods. Music will be enjoyed in London when back at my riverside house, Sandycombe Lodge, in Twickenham, made possible by my art." Indeed it was made possible because Turner designed it himself though much inspired by his friend Sir John Soane. At least he knew that his father was faithfully looking after it in his absence, and the garden including the favoured fish pond and his peacocks.

Kirkby Lonsdale, with the spectacular view of the river not only praised by Whitaker but before by Wordsworth, and later by Ruskin should have delayed him for longer were it not for the need to make another short diversion to Kendal to replenish snuff. Four days later a weary Turner arrived back to his second home near Otley with his friends.

"Hector, my friend and companion, we have a story to tell of our travels and the wonderful sights we have seen. You will rest and be cosseted now by Jenks' men in the stables."

Jenks was highly trusted as the head groom of Farnley and the riding instructor of the children. In return he and Mrs Jenks enjoyed a small cottage near to the stables.

CHAPTER 4

By now Turner was accustomed to the splendours of Farnley on this, his eighth visit since he first began to make great friendship with its owner Mr Fawkes. He could recall his skills as an architect in admiring the ancient features of Farnley, some remaining in the old wing from long before John Carr remodelled the house.

"Tell us of your travels and adventures while we dine this evening. Any traveller but you might have stayed home this summer," says Mary. "I call it a year without summer. Some say a volcano blew on the other side of the world last year. There has been so much dust in the air and crops have not grown well. If you sought grain for Hector, did it cost high? Some are even saying that the dust falling last year at Waterloo cost Napoleon his victory. If so," she concluded, "we have God as well as men to thank for his loss."

"Would that blast of nature could have been stopped as readily as our kinsman Guy was stopped from his explosive scheme in London more than two centuries ago. Not that gentlemen of the Jesuit party were all that easily stopped in those days," interjected Walter.

"But then I would have been denied the skies and the storms which are the making of my craft unless the thousands of street bonfires following have had similar effects!" added Turner slyly.

Mrs Fawkes was a kindly, even jolly soul who looked

forward to Turner's visits and made him welcome in a gentle way. For a man who had lost his mother to mental illness, and his younger sister through her death at the age of eleven, this came as a pleasing antidote to his own rather brusque manner unused to female attention.

"My good man," said Fawkes as the ladies withdrew and the wine began to flow, "We are at this moment seated on chairs made for me by Gillows when I inherited this house some twenty years ago. Had he lived to that time, they might have been made by Master Chippendale late of Otley. But he died of consumption it is said in London thirteen years before Gillows made them to their square back pattern which derives a little from a Chippendale design. No matter, the quality is of the very highest, and you are seated on best black Morocco leather from their London shop. As you know, my friend, I abhor the concept of the slave trade and made sure that Gillows were not themselves involved in that heinous work though some merchants in Lancaster were. Then I could not have invited my friend Wilberforce of Hull to be seated as you are on these chairs to debate this horror, with he and I now hoping to have released those enslaved or at least legally registered."

With the help of a little more fine wine from the Farnley cellars, Turner began to sing a song he had heard at the Sun Inn in Lancaster, sung by a sea captain recently returned from the Caribbean with ballast of fine timbers destined for Mr Gillow's workshops on the quayside. Indeed these fine timbers were to be revered by owners of Gillow furniture for 200 years because of their beautiful figuring and colour, selected by the Gillow workmen to be displayed to best advantage. No finer woods have ever been used in English furniture.

"Here's a health to honest John Bull," sang our hero

"When he is gone where will you find such another
So with hearts as with bumpers quite full
Here's a health to Old England, his mother"

By now Fawkes was joined in and the two were so noisy that Mrs Fawkes sent in a servant to see if all was well. Indeed all was *very* well. The friends talked long with the help of clay pipes. Fawkes liked to show his bluff Yorkshire character on such occasions.

"Will you return to Farnley with good speed, Turner? Mrs Fawkes and I and the children are pleased to welcome you."

"I'm planning a further tour of Europe, Fawkes, now that the wars with France are at an end. I was in Switzerland fourteen years past. Hopes of that have been dashed for years. My intent is to discover the Rhineland."

"My dear friend. I can assure you that on your return we will leave no time to see your work and commission it for this house. You will visit again, I insist. It is eight years past since you first came to Farnley, you know and we can call ourselves friends. I feel you are at home here, and for us it is good to stand aside from the social polish of London which I know you dislike even though many of your fellow artists are attracted by it."

"I do not think I am given to self-pity though I do receive some antagonism and even rejection of my work, Walter. Do you find me confident and presumptuous as some have said?"

"They should see you in your travels and in my home. I venture to say that you are more a man of the countryside than of the city," concluded Walter with a raise of his glass to his friend. "Such barbs cannot hurt you."

***

A few days later Fawkes and his shooting party were riding for the second day to Beamsley Beacon to blast more grouse out of the sky to fill the larders at Farnley and elsewhere as well as fill the game shops and provide some estate income. For Turner such action could not have been further from his life in London. He never was sure about shooting with the noise and bloodshed and found greater pleasure, not to say more relaxation when casting his line and flexing his rod on a river bank.

The ride was no more than eight or ten miles and through beautiful countryside which calmed his feelings. Could he hope to ride on a little after the sport to see the spectacular Bolton Abbey in the valley to the north west on Devonshire's land?

The chattering of the men, the downing of the ale in the shelters, and the excitement of the day would all be captured in his sketchbook.

The beaters lined up towards them as they crouched in the butts, guns ready. Turner was with Fawkes whose brother was in the next butt a few yards to the left. The grouse chack chacked overhead and swinging round with gun, Turner brought one down for the dogs to retrieve. They at least had great exercise that day.

He did not count the number of cartridges gone by the afternoon, but the number of grouse at his feet held only a small part of the lead let loose.

"It will be time to ride home..." Fawkes began to say when interrupted by a blast from the butt nearby. All they could see was a man bending over the recumbent form of Richard Hawkesworth Fawkes sprawled over the turf wall at the front of the refuge. The poor man was the victim of a ghastly accident as a gun discharged. There was shouting and demands for a litter as Fawkes and Turner steeled themselves to look closer.

"Oh my God," breathed Fawkes. "He has lost an arm and is bleeding like a pig. He must be carried to Farnley and a surgeon called." Turner busied himself getting men together to help move Richard to a hastily brought cart with a bedding of straw for some comfort and to absorb blood which could not be completely staunched with pads and strapping.

The sad party wended home slowly to cushion the poor man against jolts.

***

Turner might have stayed longer enjoying the fishing in the Wharfe had not the damnable tragedy interrupted their sport. Their ministrations were all in vain and the shooting claimed the life of Walter's brother the next day.

He stayed for a further few days to help the family as he might. Never had his amusements for the children been more apposite as he attempted to shield them from all that was going on around them in the house. Then it was back to London, to try to put the event behind him. Teaching perspective at the Academy did not give him much relief but thankfully some respite could be had from starting to paint from his dozens of sketches to satisfy his publisher, at last.

CHAPTER 5

With more than a year passed, Turner turned to his agent.

"Griffin, ensure that my small painting of High Cup Nick is not included in those to go to Longmans and for engraving. It is a commission for Lord Thanet at Appleby Castle. I go to Fawkes's again next week and shall take it to deliver. I cannot delay to return to my beloved North of England and spectacular scenes for my sketches, this time in Richmondshire. As you know, since my coming of age, my visits to Farnley have been every year. I'm pleased to count Fawkes and Parker at Browsholme now as my friends as well as clients and even Lascelles at Harewood chooses to buy my work."

By now Turner could cope easily with the three-day coach journey to Farnley via Grantham, Doncaster and Leeds because he so much enjoyed looking forward to returning to his beloved northern counties, seeing his friends again. Most of his acquaintances in London thought of him as rather dour and even unexciting. But they had not seen him in his other guise as traveller, fisherman, gunman and his sheer dedication to his sketching. Even if they had, they would have been utterly astounded to see him playing with and entertaining the Fawkes children since he was never to have any legitimate ones of his own. He found more companionship and pleasure with children of his lovers and friends than ever he did with the society people and Academicians who sought his company now that he had become one of them.

***

Transfer to Fawkes's gig at Otley soon speeded him to Farnley. He could not be allowed to drive lest he reinforced his nickname in the family of 'the over-Turner'.

Though welcomed as always by Fawkes seniors, it was to the children that William turned almost as he entered the house. For their part, there was great excitement to see him again.

"Please, sir," spoke Hawkey, ably supported by young Richard. "Please sir, may we watch you paint birds again for the album to be ours when we reach enough years for us to own it?"

The enthusiasm of youth was amply matched by its acquisitiveness. But it was Turner's delight to be captured for this task. He always left a stash of papers and brushes for this very project and was glad to escape from conversation while he painted. Even the children were quiet as they watched exquisite details of feathers in wonderful colours appear as he added them to his drawings.

That evening, before the fire the men re-warmed their friendship.

"Tell me of your tour of the lowlands since last we spoke," begged Fawkes.

"I shall not complete my paintings this year," responded Turner and, as Fawkes well knew, Turner's eloquence came from his hand, not his mouth. It took persuasion by the older man to get a brief summary of his friend's travel in Belgium, Germany and Holland. In truth he wished to place his name against those paintings which would emerge, to hang in his

London house. That agreed, they turned to the contents of the cellar below, Fawkes's tobacco and Turner's snuff.

In characteristic haste, Turner soon rushed to prepare again for his next tour.

"May I beg you Fawkes to speed this watercolour to Thanet at Appleby whilst I travel and sketch in the country of Richmond? He desired it when I visited him there two summers ago. I shall be pleased if Thanet delights in this painting. I hold it in my mind with my depiction in oils of *Snow storm in the Alps* some five years ago.

"I believe it captures the storm of that day in the Pennine hills better than any of my works in the north of the country. I feel that it imitates nature in a manner not reached by the art of realism, myself included in my earlier work. It should not be seen as a description, but as my lasting impression of that moment. Thus I used a light palette. For that I prefer to work in watercolour for it is fluid and quick."

"I like your conversation my friend," said Fawkes warmly. "You so seldom give of your own feelings for your work. That you have done so here will surely make this picture one to be cherished one day by its future owners. It is a forerunner of modernity and I wish it were mine."

"I shall be well pleased, Joseph. I have not dined and taken wine with Thanet for some time and it is said that he may not be long in Appleby. Mrs Fawkes, do you recall that writing slope we had from Mr Gillow in Lancaster a few years before the new century? I wish to see if it will take Mr Turner's painting in its drawer to keep it sound on its journey to Appleby with me. I have need of a journey to Castle Bolton to see my friend Scrope and I can ride on from there."

"We have not used it now that we don't travel so much, so

I had it taken by a servant to the attic rooms," she replied, "I will send for it."

***

In this way the friends parted and safety for the painting was assured. For Fawkes it was not a question of its monetary value, but of the skill with which his friend could capture the atmosphere and character of the scenes which he committed to paper and canvass. He had no equal.

PART 2

Tempora mutantur
Anon

CHAPTER 6

Two centuries later, Edward Dendron and his wife were celebrating their silver wedding anniversary. One objective was to see Eric Shanes's wonderfully curated *Turner Watercolours* at the Royal Academy. Having been completely overcome as a young man by the Turner exhibition at the Tate in 1974-5, Edward had convinced himself that no other British artist could compare with Turner in capturing the atmosphere of landscapes and skies tinged with light and colour or obscured by storm clouds.

Edward much later had become a keen minor collector of good, but fairly ordinary English watercolours when he could find them at modest prices and especially if they depicted landscapes which he knew. In his case this frequently meant Northern England and was perhaps a way of reminding himself of his origins there. He was proud that his unusual family name came from their descent in the tiny ancient village of Dendron close to Barrow-in-Furness and known as Dene in the Domesday Book, perhaps as a reference to deer sheltering there. He had been taught that the celebrated portrait painter, George Romney who was raised nearby, attended the tiny village school there for a short time in the mid eighteenth century, perhaps its main claim to fame. It stirred in Edward a growing appreciation of fine art.

Though his father was an engineer at the Barrow shipyards Edward was much more bookish, encouraged by his mother, a librarian in the nearby small town of Dalton-in-

Furness. Later at secondary school in Dalton and as a consequence of the town name, he grew up acutely aware of the background forty miles north near Cockermouth of John Dalton the eminent scientist and pioneer of atomic theory. For Edward as a boy, atomic theory was largely incomprehensible but it kept reminding him of the nuclear threat of the early nineteen sixties when the Kruschev-Kennedy confrontation over delivery of missiles to Cuba terrified everyone. But his engineer father talked more of the development of nuclear power in nearby Winscale, or Sellafield as it is known now.

In truth Edward was far more attracted to that other son of Cockermouth, William Wordsworth. Like the poet, Edward was essentially an outdoor man himself and in his youth had greatly enjoyed exploring on foot parts of the Lake District on his doorstep rather than the even closer coastal sands three or four miles down the road. Of course he knew Furness Abbey, one of the most beautiful ruins in England for it too was a mere three miles of cycling from home. He found his freedom and inspiration more on the open fells than in the valleys, though he recognised their beauty at least as much as do car visitors today. Curiously enough in that appreciation, he was literally following not only in Wordsworth's footsteps but also those of John Dalton. Also like him, he sought education in Kendal where Edward became articled to a local solicitor. Perhaps both would have preferred to stay in the vicinity of those mountains, but for both, advancement had meant moves south.

As the centre of gravity of the economy changed with the move from heavy engineering to the provision of services and with it a geographical shift in opportunities, Edward, like many, had drifted towards London. He might have returned to Lancashire after establishing himself as a moderately successful small-town solicitor were it not for having met

Rhoda, the girl who was to become his wife and companion and who was a daughter of the Home Counties. Now in his mid sixties he prided himself on having kept in good enough physical condition to still enjoy walking, albeit at a slower pace and rarely in mountains. Fairly slight in build, he still stood very upright and covered the ground at an energetic pace, whether he was in town or in country.

He had never really completely lost his northern accent, nor his willingness to 'call a spade a spade, or a shovel, in his vocabulary.'

Rhoda came from a somewhat more comfortable background in Essex; a small village just to the north of Colchester. As a girl she had been taken with her sister to see the wonderful old buildings of Lavenham and the classic countryside of Constable's paintings across the county boundary in Suffolk.

Her main exercise had been cycling along small country lanes. That meant learning how to fix a puncture and occasionally to fix the bike. She became conscious of a real interest in things mechanical and practical and liked to hang about her dad's garden shed where he had tools and the hobby of woodwork, even a little carving when he could get suitable wood. For his part he was happy to teach her to use the tools.

She had hardly heard of Turner. Why should she, living so near to the playground of his contemporary and occasional critic Master John Constable? Life was quite comfortable, she thought, in a middle-class family surrounded by a modest level of affluence built up after memories of the War years and rationing had begun to fade.

In her teenage years she still had little knowledge of people or places much north of East Anglia. That had begun to change in her early twenties when she met Edward by sheer

45

chance, in the home of the Wallace Collection in London's Manchester Square. They were in the city for different reasons. Edward because one of his clients had had a minor motoring accident there and he wanted to see the scene of it for himself, the better to represent him. Even better if he could find the time to explore a part of the city which he didn't know. Rhoda was there to see her younger sister Sarah take up her place at the College of Nursing in Henrietta Street. They had both gravitated to the Wallace partly because entry was free, but mainly to escape the threat of heavy rain. It was a new experience for both of them to enter one of London's surviving great houses. By lunchtime they were ready to find a snack in the museum cafe in the days long before the courtyard had been covered over and taking luncheon there had become something of a social thing.

Now they looked back on it as the place where they had exchanged views on the ostentatious interiors, the grandeur of a London town house and the price of lunch.

But to last them until now were the stirrings of lifetime interests in furniture for Rhoda, and paintings for Edward; in neither case in the largely Baroque French exhibits there but in the more prosaic English styles a little more suited to their backgrounds. Edward generally gravitated towards Impressionism in any gallery but was enjoying its Turner and Bonington watercolours. Rhoda was more interested in the furniture though her taste was not for the ornate French styles dominant here. But she did admire the workmanship, especially of the important collection of Boulle pieces. Both admired quality when they saw it, and by the mid afternoon had thought that they might find it in each other.

Indeed they did.

CHAPTER 7

The story of them together begins thirty years later after that momentous meeting at the Wallace.

The Dendrons came from that extremely fortunate generation born shortly after the War with opportunities for wider access to higher education, and perhaps more stable employment with reasonable, even comfortable incomes. To them there seemed to be no need, and certainly no wish, to educate family privately, even if they could have afforded to do so. Alongside these privileges Rhoda and Edward had taken advantage of the extra access to the English countryside which wider car ownership had made so desirable to families from fairly ordinary, though often very imaginative and intelligent backgrounds. They had greatly enjoyed the pleasures and occasional pain of seeing their boys mature and make their own lives, first at home, and now in their own careers after university. This was before fees and consequent debts became mandatory. As parents they had paid off their mortgage some time ago before worrying increases in property prices had been driven by overseas investment in the region, low interest rates and encouragement to debt. Both remembered the introduction of 'Hire Purchase' or 'Never Never' contracts enabling wider access to material goods, but like their own parents had not liked the idea of borrowing except for a house. Like many of their generation they had saved and could relax a little, looking forward to comfortable pension support later. But Edward and

Rhoda knew and had anticipated for some time that their own children, let alone their grandchildren might not enjoy these same privileges. They felt that a balance had to be struck between trying to take this into account, perhaps by making some savings or even by setting up small trusts for the grandchildren, whilst achieving a modest but reasonable lifestyle for themselves. Neither had inherited much in wealth or privilege.

They felt that they had been able to arrive at à point where their budgeting might allow modest investment in the art they both so much loved. Both preferred the more permanent pleasures which they hoped this offered, rather than a similar amount spent on extra holidays though they did enjoy some travel including occasional river cruises. Another ambition was to share their hobbies a little bit with grandchildren. Remembering his background, Edward dreamt of tramping the northern fells with them, perhaps as three-generation expeditions. For her part, Rhoda had visions of the children finding pleasure in cycling both as a means of responsible transport and of enjoyment. Perhaps they would even treasure the few pieces of handsome old furniture passing through her shop which she had retained. They might one day inherit them along with Edward's nice watercolours. None of these objects were particularly valuable except as good examples of their time. She sometimes said that with prospects of a reasonably long retirement these days, she and Edward could look forward to the future whilst living alongside a few reminders from the past. Fundamentally they were a forward-looking couple and enjoyed exploring the geography of Britain and its history sometimes shared with friends and family. Friends, however, who they felt lucky to meet regularly. Funny how, for the young, screen contact seemed to be replacing face to face conversation. A huge social change they thought, in less than one generation – the millennial kids they had heard them called. But then families were now so much more dispersed.

Yet Edward and Rhoda also knew that their grandchildren would have so much to enjoy in a rapidly changing world as they grew up, rather than thinking of living in the past. Like most generations the Dendrons felt that the future held many challenges for their children, though they wondered if they would have been able to meet that challenge themselves. They had confidence that what they perceived to have been material and social improvement in their own lifetimes would continue in some ways because they had faith in the next generation to ensure this. Being highly adaptable seemed to be the crucial characteristic of a twenty-first century life.

They were doing their best now to adapt to future retirement, they hoped. It was nice to have up-to-date domestic facilities and comforts alongside a few old objects to admire and treasure as well as use daily. Bit by bit they were also learning to use the new technologies, often with a little help from the boys and grandchildren.

***

As they approached retirement Edward and Rhoda had come to enjoy a happy lifestyle in their modest home in Berkhamsted from where they could access the fine museums and galleries of the capital city, but without quite the means to match aspiration. They had always taken the view that enjoying seeing fine works of art and beautiful objects need not lead to a wish to own them. However, now that Edward had enjoyed some success as a provincial solicitor in the town and Rhoda ran her small antiques business up the road from his office, they could permit themselves a little more freedom in their ambitions of actual ownership of a few nice objects.

They were relaxing in their nice house overlooking the canal with its quiet narrowboats passing by at a stately four miles per hour. They frequently walked along the towpath, enabling exchanges of greetings with people on the boats and admiring the colourful décor of many of them, including quaint bargemen's kettles and the like. Just across on the other side from the towpath was the ancient castle ruin providing a fine backcloth to their view. It was an evening conducive to reflecting on their lifestyle as they approached retirement. It was often a topic of conversation for them; not always strictly seriously.

"As long as we prefer rabbiting on to skiing," Rhoda suddenly said, apparently irrelevantly.

"I don't quite follow that remark," came from Edward.

"Of course you've heard what skiing is these days, Edward, Spending the Kids Inheritance."

"And rabbiting on?"

"Retaining a Bit By Investment Trusts," she ventured with a smile, pleased with her invention.

"At least most of the cash we have saved over the years has come from taxed earned income so we needn't feel too guilty if some of that can benefit the kids through a trust," Edward remarked.

"Gaining from inflated Property Prices is another matter. Is that GIPPing? Perhaps the Chancellor of the Exchequer prefers skiing on the ground that it boosts the economy now and generates extra taxes. Now it's me that is rabbiting on," he conceded.

"My goodness, Rhoda. Those G and Ts haven't half led to some amateur philosophy. Maybe because they were hardly half measures."

All this was symptomatic of their joint appreciation of wordplay.

Perhaps this somewhat juvenile sense of humour had morphed into Edward's rather infuriating habit of punning which Rhoda had grown up to consider the lowest form of wit rather than Oscar Wilde's perhaps equal claim for sarcasm.

She couldn't help feeling a bit superior as she recalled her rather more sheltered childhood days. But perhaps it gave Edward some respite from a career in which words had to have unambiguous meanings even if occurring in largely unpunctuated sentences.

They ended the afternoon in reciprocal chuckles which were not entirely a product of pre-prandial intake.

CHAPTER 8

A week or two later, both had the prospect of a restful day. Edward was up to date with his client's business and Rhoda could shut up shop for a few hours.

"Do you fancy a day in the city, doing one or two of the museums?" suggested Rhoda. They decided on a morning in the British Museum where there was a special exhibition of loans from the new Egyptian museum in Luxor. It was hugely nostalgic for they had spent their silver wedding anniversary on the Misra, a wonderful steam-driven boat on the Nile. Edward had chosen it because he had discovered that it was built in Preston; not a million miles from his boyhood home. King Farouk had it converted for his personal use and now it was a small, rather exclusive vessel for tourists. They had had a wonderful trip before the outbreak of terrorism which damaged the tourism industry, and with it a sizeable proportion of the Egyptian economy.

Luxor was perhaps their favourite stopping point because it embraced the temples of Karnak and Luxor as well as, of course, the Valley of the Kings on the other side of the river. They had been transported in more than one sense as Rhoda had packed Agatha Christie for the journey. Both enjoyed a bit of mystery in their reading, especially when associated with a location they knew.

After a fascinating morning transported on the Nile in their fertile imaginations, they retired to the cafe in the museum courtyard. They soon reminded themselves that the wonderful space visible over the rims of their coffee cups could not be seen by the ordinary visitor some twenty years before. They knew that it had contained the stacks of books hidden behind the galleries of the round reading room. Not until these were transported with enormous, but unsung human effort to the new British Library at St Pancras was it revealed and so beautifully restored by Norman Foster.

It provided a very restful atmosphere for them to reflect over lunch on how life had developed for them since that meeting at the Wallace and to consider how much their tastes might have changed in the meantime.

***

Neither Rhoda nor Edward was particularly demonstrative but it was abundantly clear from their affectionate glances that they were a very loving couple with a deep understanding of each other gained in so many years.

Rhoda enjoyed teasing Edward about his choice of fine art. As a solicitor, she thought of him as wedded to precise facts rather than opinions, to logic rather than sentiment. But he had come to greatly admire the work of the Impressionists. Nevertheless as a man she loved him for precisely those intangible qualities especially when they led him to his lifetime's appreciation of dramatic landscapes in reality and their representation by those few artists who in his judgement could capture them on paper or canvas. For his part Edward admired Rhoda's ability to see and respect high quality design and artisanship in more practical items of everyday from small treen to household furniture. Quietly he felt rather humbled by her superior craft skills.

Perhaps as a result of carrying out small repairs to her stock in the shop, it was Rhoda who enjoyed DIY and spent time in her little workshop shed reviving memories of her father's at the bottom of his garden. Although self-taught, since those days she had mastered the use of woodworking tools. As a consequence she understood the very high level of skill required for cabinet making.

They both judged art and design by whether they felt they could live with and enjoy if it came their way. Perhaps, she sometimes thought, that might explain why their taste had not embraced postmodernism. With their simplistic views they certainly did not feel that they would like their home to be adorned by some of the installations of today, such as a Tracey Emin bed. Rhoda permitted herself an ironic smile as she said:

"Maybe it would be controversial to recall Francois Truffaut's dictum that 'Airing one's dirty linen never makes for a masterpiece'!"

Perhaps its place would always be in a museum. Of course they understood that some of the avant garde of today would be the desiderata of tomorrow, and some would come to convey a sense of enormous progress and challenge of the status quo. A few might even meet the eventual test of time.

Edward reflected on whether Turner would today have won the Turner Prize. Try as he would, he could not imagine his hero planning an installation, despite the painter's admiration for architectural constructions. With a chuckle he guessed that Whistler would certainly not have won it if John Ruskin had been one of the judges.

***

"Well I enjoyed that snack and time to reflect," confessed Edward, "even if we did dream a little."

Rhoda came back to earth when she remembered her other mission for the day.

"May I leave you Edward for the afternoon, whilst I take myself off to the viewing of fine English furniture to be auctioned later this week at Bonhams? I get so little chance to see superb period pieces, especially English," she said.

"Of course, my dear," said Edward a little hesitantly, for he rather feared the pressures and risks of auctions.

"Bring the catalogue back with you and we can enjoy mulling over it when we get back home." He generously added that she might choose what to bid for as long as it was within their means.

"Pity it isn't a sale of paintings. They take up so much less space than a Pembroke table or even a Georgian mirror."

Her departure gave Edward a chance to indulge his increasing passion for Turner. Remembering the display of Turner's possessions which as a teenager he had seen on loan from the BM to the exhibition of Turner and his life at the Tate, he resolved to ask if he could see the Turner bequest.

"Blow it," he realised, "I'd forgotten that the Turner bequest was eventually transferred permanently from here to the Tate."

With that they went their separate ways for the afternoon.

An hour later, Edward had secured permission to see parts of the Turner material. He was fascinated by the sketchbooks, particularly, of course, those recording their owner's visits to the North of England.

CHAPTER 9

In the evening they sat down to brief each other on their afternoon's experiences. It was warm enough to sit in the conservatory in rather comfortable rattan chairs with nice cushions from the shop in the high street. Rhoda kicked off her walking shoes in favour of fur-lined slippers.

"I think," she said when Edward had placed a box of his favourite chocolates on the coffee table, "that seeing such wonderful expressions of human endeavour which today you have seen in fine art and I have seen made in wood is quite uplifting. It suggests to me that having a concept in mind is one thing, but having the skill to make it as a tangible thing brings together mind and hand which few can achieve."

***

"Rhoda, dear, I have had the most exciting idea today whilst looking again at Turner's life and work. You know, even Ruskin, not noted for his appreciation of 'avant garde' painters, saw Turner as painting 'the true, the beautiful and the intellectual', a compliment indeed from a man who had Whistler drummed out of the country to exile in Venice ostensibly for his... *daubs*. I could never understand how Ruskin could not appreciate at least the earlier works of Whistler whilst being such a strong admirer of Turner. In my view there is a lot of the impressionist in Turner, long before they existed and Whistler imbibed their skills in Paris before coming to London. Perhaps Ruskin was more influenced by Victorian views of morality in art – even created them – rather than the art itself. Though he would surely never admit that. At least his advocate and protégé Burne-Jones could see in Whistler 'an unrivalled appreciation of atmosphere and beautiful colour, especially in moonlight scenes'."

"I wouldn't go as far as that!" continued Edward. "He could have been talking about Turner himself. I reckon Turner was *the* first of the Impressionists and very much better at his craft than many later included under that banner, certainly than Whistler!" At least Edward had been stimulated to think about these men, though he had no idea what modern critics would say, or even if he was right about his assertions.

"Anyway, enough of that and back to my idea," he said. "Do you know, I discovered today that Turner made sketches on his northern tour in 1816 at High Cup Nick – you remember, that amazing place the boys told us of visiting on their walking holiday in Yorkshire and Cumbria some years ago, and which really excited them. I never had a chance to see it when I was growing up.

"Well, I have today seen two sketches by him looking down the valley across to the Lake District mountains from the Nick. But, and here's the point, there are no known paintings of either of them. I feel I can't rest until I have completely satisfied myself that no painting exists. Granted, the sketches look as if they must have been soaked and dried out, but he often made wonderful paintings from the most rudimentary of his drawings. From what the boys said, the location is so wild and atmospheric that I find it difficult to believe that he didn't attempt to make these sketches into a final painting. His whole being responded to experiences like that – think of his 'snow storm, avalanche and inundation in Piedmont' of 1836 and of course, the storm surrounding 'Hannibal and his army crossing the Alps', not to mention 'Steam boat off a harbour's mouth'. He absolutely revelled in being in the midst of extreme weather and recording it in a way which no other artist has achieved. Perhaps that is why he came to so much treasure his trips to the North of England. He would certainly find tough weather there which helped to fashion not only the landscape but the men, that is the labourers who did so much to found the wealth of this country."

As he built up his argument, Edward was getting rather excited about his proposition. He paused to consider the impact of his next statement. He knew the dictum that timing is everything, but was equally aware that in this instance he was almost exactly 200 hundred years out of date.

"Could there be an unknown painting waiting to be discovered? Wouldn't it be exciting to try to search for one?"

With that he triumphantly concluded his thesis and sat down.

Almost reading his mind, Rhoda interjected:

"Two centuries have passed since he trod those parts: during which scholars have poured over his diaries and sketches. You really are a bit of a romantic at heart. What makes you think that you can succeed in finding one where others have failed?"

"I think it possible that no one has even tried," riposted Edward. "It is pretty well agreed that he didn't make paintings of those sketches. After all they were not part of his commission from Longmans though he did some wonderful paintings of nearby sites such as High Force and Cauldron

Snout whilst on that same journey.

"The sketches are rudimentary and the place is not on everyone's bucket list!"

***

"I'm going to put the kettle on," Rhoda announced. "Would you care for an Earl Grey?"

A typical English action that in the midst of absorbing Edward's great idea, Rhoda chose to make a brew.

While she was pottering about in the kitchen Edward took a chance to snaffle another of his favourite chocolates from the box which seemed to spend a lot more time on his side of the table than on Rhoda's. His thoughts were leaping ahead.

"I'm serving up in the sitting room," Rhoda shouted. "It's getting a bit chilly for me out there."

Grabbing the chocolates, Edward followed her through. Two cups of Earl Grey were enough for him to formulate his plan.

"I think an answer might lie in the North. What say we go up there and have a scout around? It would be a great holiday to stay perhaps in Appleby, to explore and meet people to see if any rumours exist. Are you game? I'll need to get access again to his diaries to follow his itinerary. Even if I am letting my imagination run riot about an unknown painting, it would be very enjoyable to see those counties which he tramped in the old palatinates of the historic North. It's surprising that we haven't already been. But there are so many sights around here to relish with the more benign qualities of the rolling landscapes, glades and villages of the lowland counties, not least Constable Country. It most surely has the 'power to chasten and subdue.'"

"Well, Edward, when you have finished quoting that wonderful wordsmith of the North, Wordsworth, I wonder if we might do a deal? Which I'll come to in a minute."

It was her turn to talk about the day's adventures.

***

Rhoda planted the catalogue in front of him and began to leaf through it.

"Like you, I've had a great day, myself, viewing the sale rooms. Look at this superb cheveret made by Gillows of Lancaster, on page 33, Lot 104."

"What on earth is a cheveret, Rhoda? It sounds like a small American car!"

"Don't be so daft, Edward," said Rhoda between chuckles. "An educated man like you ought to recognise its use for a small writing desk. I had a most interesting chat with one of the Bonhams' staff who really was enthusiastic about it. Veneered in satinwood with exquisite tulipwood banding. It doesn't have the original writing surface which would have been baize, I suppose, but it does have original ivory knobs on the small drawers and beautiful brass handles on the main one. Anyone looking at it would say 'Sheraton' though apparently there is quite a bit of doubt about the extent to which Sheraton designs were always new, or copied from existing pieces made by craftsmen like those at Gillows. Would you believe it, it turns out that this company made pieces of that quality for over 200 years, long before and after Sheraton's time, for the gentry, the aristocracy, not just here, but with a thriving export market to the colonies? He told me that the company archives have survived after being more or less inaccessible until 1964 when a retiring director of what was by then Waring & Gillow found them in a loft in their building in Lancaster. He donated them to the Westminster City Library. That's the reason why individual items can sometimes not only be identified as 'Gillow', but even traced to the original design drawing, the precise journeyman or team who made it, the costings of the materials and sometimes correspondence with the purchaser. They apparently had an outlet in Oxford Street as well as their base in Lancaster. I wonder if I could get permission to see those archives? There are two or three photographic copies on microfilm, he said. He also advised me that if visiting the North West I could see such exquisite pieces at museums in Lancaster, Kendal and at National Trust Tatton Park in Cheshire."

***

Now it was Rhoda's turn to make a proposal.

"Could you be persuaded to take one or two of these places in on your way to explore your crazy idea about High Cup Nick? There are Turners to be seen at Abbot Hall Gallery in Kendal," she rather cheekily slipped in, knowing that the gallery also displayed fine Gillow pieces looking very much at home in their Georgian surroundings. The biggest prize of all for her might also be the inclusion of Leighton Hall near Lancaster, the ancestral home of the Gillow family not unexpectedly furnished in eponymous style.

"That splendid man at Bonhams has been more effective than any travel agent in convincing me to plead, Edward, for a joint adventure well north of Watford Gap."

"My goodness", thought Edward, "I'm getting boxed in," though he secretly was rather delighted with Rhoda's enthusiasm for the trip.

"In point of fact it will be pretty amusing to plan and there just might be some rather comfortable country house hotels to welcome us on route. I believe that the Whitworth Gallery in Manchester has a fine collection of Turners. How's that for a Northern Powerhouse?" he added, echoing current political thinking. In point of fact they both enjoyed holidays with a clear objective and if they could combine each of their interests, so much the better. This time they would be exploring parts of the country completely new to Rhoda and bringing back old memories to Edward.

"Well I'm going to do my homework on Gillow and you can do yours on Turner," said Rhoda, more than satisfied with the turn of Edward's thinking. She was well versed in the art of meeting him halfway and even supporting his half of a debate if it led to equanimity and plans for action.

***

What was secretly exciting Rhoda, as she thought about the furniture she had seen, was the sudden realisation of how creative was its design and making. Although hardly any commentator would not think of the fine arts and literature as being highly creative and cultured, there seemed to her to be less agreement about the great creativity of making objects, or even of less tangible things like the forming of a hypothesis by a scientist, the design of experiments to test it and the skill in writing about it.

"How many highly creative technologists and scientists

let alone furniture makers are household names?" she reflected.

"Designers, yes, but perhaps only three: Chippendale, Hepplewhite and Sheraton, curiously all from the North of England, though later needing to seek their fortunes in London. But who remembers those wonderfully skilled journeymen who made the pieces by transforming those sketches into a beautiful object? To own one would not just be to use a table or chair, but to admire and treasure it through generations as a work of art of the highest order as well as being a functional object."

Then back to earth as she considered her proposal.

"Of course I would expect that satinwood cheveret to go for far more than I could possibly bid," confessed Rhoda, "but there is another eighteenth-century Gillow piece, this time a portable writing desk at which I am considering having a go. It would be fun to try." She did have experience of bidding at low-key auctions with not much at stake. But Bonhams of London was quite another matter!

"Tell me more," spluttered a slightly worried Edward, who was always more cautious than Rhoda when it came to the frisson of the auction room.

"Don't panic, love," confirmed Rhoda, "I shall fix my upper limit before even entering the building and I won't go over it, no matter what. After all, I don't need to allow for making a profit on re-sale as I do in my role as a small dealer, or even to think of it as an investment. It would be for our personal enjoyment and maybe even for future generations of Dendrons."

"Mind you don't get caught out by phone bidders pushing up the price quickly. And don't forget to factor in the buyer's premium," cautioned Edward. "Anyway. what is it?"

"You know the kind of thing," she began to explain. "We've both seen the writing slope on display at the British Library, owned by Jane Austen. Well this one is so much better quality and design than that one made in Winchester apparently for her 19th birthday. If I had one of those there is no knowing how my letter writing to the grandchildren might improve!"

"I thought most people wrote e-mails these days, and most children have the means and skills to do it," muttered Edward who despite his rather conservative nature wasn't a complete Luddite, particularly when it came to the convenience and speed of e-mails.

"Of course you are right," agreed Rhoda "but think of the fun and indeed utter pleasure when you and I went through your parents' stuff and found real letters between them and their Victorian grandparents in their own handwriting and own signatures. Would you think of throwing those away without reading them as you might a few memory sticks or whatever, wondering if they could be accessed easily fifty years from now?"

"Humph," came from the armchair on the other side of the wood-burning stove. "I thought we were on the subject of bidding for a box made a couple of hundred years ago. Is it big enough to carry a tablet when we are travelling?" he joked.

"Well it's bigger than Jane Austen's one, so I should be able to write longer letters than she did between Darcy and Elizabeth," chuckled Rhoda. "Seriously, just think how satisfactory it could be to own an object of such interest and quality, and imagine what documents might have been written on its green baize surface. Everything about it is original, you know, even the little glass ink containers. It has the most beautiful colour of Spanish mahogany. I like it even better to call it Hispaniola wood. It sounds so romantic after the ship of that name. It will become my 'treasure' if I can get it. The key thing is that it has the Gillow impression on either side of the lock – 'Gillows' on one side, and 'Gillows' slightly skewed above 'Lancaster' on the other; the oldest known stamps used by the company from the 1790s.

"You win," spoke the armchair. "Clearly you have really fallen for it and that's the very best reason to bid, not any investment value it might or might not have."

Secretly he was delighted to see his dear wife so enthusiastic and really hoped she would be successful. In point of fact she was the more adventurous of the two.

CHAPTER 10

"Shall I go to the auction on my own?" mused Rhoda when the day had dawned for her ordeal. "Yes, I think that would be best. In some ways I'd like Edward's support but I don't think I could bear him sitting next to me if I failed. I'd rather recover first and explain later."

"I'm off to London," she shouted to the bathroom door. "You can have a quiet day. There's a pizza in the freezer and I'll be back before supper."

***

Rhoda felt a bit intimidated, even panicky as she entered the splendid rooms of Bonhams again after her initial viewing earlier in the week. Her first task was to register as a bidder and then to have another look at Lot 52 before it was taken away for the last time from the viewing room. There it was on top of a nice Pembroke table. It wasn't in her nature to be mysterious but she felt that sidling up to it and trying not to look interested in case another potential bidder was eyeing it was the thing to do. It felt quite cloak and dagger! Perhaps it would be a little less desirable to the other bidders than some of the other spectacular pieces in the room, she hoped. But what about that tall chap over there in the tweed jacket who she imagined was playing a similar game? Or that young woman in spectacles with the William Morris shawl and the mobile attached to her ear? Was she phoning her partner for advice on Lot 52?

"I've got to concentrate on the job in hand," she insisted to herself, "or I'll never make it in one piece to the bidding room. Best thing to try to look relaxed and confident as if it doesn't matter to me either way."

But really she knew it did matter to her. It was a piece of history and her imagination was already conjuring up visions of sea captains or even a general or two writing correspondence or instructions on its slope which might alter the course of history, or at least the course of a ship!

The time came to go through to the bidding room. Rhoda settled in to her chosen chair about two thirds of the way back where she had judged that the auctioneer would see her clearly, and that she could see many of her competing bidders ahead.

There were fewer people in the bidding room than Rhoda expected, but an ominous row of assistants with telephones on the right hand of the auctioneer. It seemed a lifetime as business progressed through dozens of precious items, none of them really registering with her as she tensely waited.

***

"Lot 52," called the rather urbane auctioneer. "A very fine example of a writing slope by Gillows of Lancaster. Late eighteenth century, George III. Totally original with all fittings and contents as supplied. Property of a gentleman. May I say one thousand pounds? I have 1,250 over there… thank you, a telephone bid for fifteen hundred…"

Rhoda tried to sense if bidding was slowing a little. It was still within her limit when she raised her paddle to the auctioneer and two bids later it was hers! Had she really got it? Could it really, really have been knocked down to her? She felt a little weak and that she could have been knocked down… with a feather, not an auctioneer's mallet.

***

At home, Edward was settling down to watch the Belgian Grand Prix from Spa, which he had recorded. It seems strange that he allowed himself the pleasure of watching a sport seemingly completely at odds with his rather calm demeanour and general appreciation of the peace of the countryside. Perhaps it had something to do with his feeling of pride that, although owned by mainly European ventures, many of the cars appeared to be developed and built within about fifty miles of his home here in Berkhamsted and the world champion came from his adopted county? Then there was his upbringing by an engineer father. He could appreciate the skill and courage involved as he watched seventeen cars hurtling into the chicane at Eau Rouge, with three not having made it past turn one. At least Hamilton was through. Even with the sound turned down a bit, these twenty-first-century cars filled the room with screaming engines. But not a patch on Rhoda's scream from the front door and all the way up the hallway.

"Good heavens," Edward said to himself. "I'll bet she's got it. It's definitely a shout of success, not a cry of failure."

One look at her face and he knew he was right. She could hardly get off her coat before she was rushing over to his arms in sheer joy. The strain of trying to look calm until all arrangements had concluded at Bonhams, trying to stop fidgeting on the train home had taken its toll.

"Well where is it then?" said Edward, then with a sudden doubt, "Is it the writing box you have got or the cheveret?"

"No need to panic," smiled Rhoda, "I would have had to drop out long before that reached its peak. It went for twice the top estimate. No, I am now the proud owner of a Gillow portable writing desk. It's jolly heavy actually and it has to be removed from the Bonhams store in the next few days to avoid storage charges. Do you think I might persuade you to drive up with me to get it?"

Usually Edward heartily disliked having to drive in central London, the more so since the introduction of the congestion charge, though he approved of it. At least he didn't feel too bad about taking in their hybrid car.

"Will it fit all right in the car?" he anxiously asked.

"Oh yes," the answer came immediately. "Don't think I haven't been mentally measuring up everything on my way home." Secretly Edward couldn't wait to see her prize.

***

Three days later, the prize was at home in Berkhamsted. Unlike most objects in the house, the freshly installed writing slope was now of little or no practical use except to remind the Dendrons of past design and elegant workmanship. In its day it facilitated writing on the move in much the same way as a laptop or tablet. Rhoda still hadn't got over the novelty and enjoyment of such features as the concealed lock mechanism for the drawer, hidden until the box itself was unlocked and opened. When admiring the construction of the drawer with its fine dovetails Rhoda was turning it over near the window when she spotted on its underside a pencilled signature: W

Naylor. She could easily imagine the craftsman taking his pencil from its convenient perch on his ear when the box was finished, to take some ownership of his highly skilled labour. Just like her father used to do. She felt closer to the box's history as a consequence of this exciting find.

CHAPTER 11

"If you are thinking that I might join you hiking up to this place in Cumbria which sounds like the Devil raising his glass to somebody," joked Rhoda, "I think I'm going to have to get into training a bit."

"I assume you are referring to High Cup Nick," spluttered Edward.

"I'd thought of that. We can easily get a bit of uphill from Berkhamsted centre onto Ash Ridge. We've often walked along the ridge after parking the car, haven't we? But it would be a good test to do it from town, perhaps five or six miles the round trip and downhill all the way coming back?" he added by way of encouragement. Rhoda thought longingly of her bike on which she was much more accustomed to taking her exercise. But it is pretty hilly in and around Berko. And she found herself feeling increasingly envious of the new electric bikes.

"We could set off by the castle and past the cricket field, I think. Better go on a day when there isn't a match on. I think I might get sidetracked. When we've walked along the ridge the National Trust cafe will be all the more acceptable to break the journey."

"What about proper footwear and clothing?" was Rhoda's first thought, soon expressed to Edward. Knowing her practical bent, he had no difficulty persuading her that strong trainers would be OK for the Ash Ridge expedition and weather was unlikely to be a major factor. However, he advised that for the trip north, useful mountain gear was best bought near mountain territory where the shopkeepers were often practising mountaineers themselves and could advise from experience. They would not be concerned with fashion so much as reliability of use.

"I suggest that we kit ourselves out in the shops of somewhere like Lancaster or in the Lake District itself when we travel north."

***

Back home with the kettle on, and sharing their experiences on the walk, Rhoda thought of these stories written by a local man, Graham Greene, and even pictured one on a certain portable desk with its reading ledge on which to prop it. She was a great reader.

"Edward, I came across a very curious fact when I was in the library the other day. You have your abiding interest in J. M. W. Turner and I'm beginning to get interested in the Gillow family. The near coincidence is that Turner's dates are 1775 to 1851 and Richard Gillow the second, grandson of the company founder Robert, was born in 1772 and died in 1849. They were almost exact contemporaries but living 250 miles apart. Perhaps less of a coincidence for creative men of the time, they both studied architecture, Richard bringing those skills to bear not only on furniture design but on building design as well. As far as I know Turner enjoyed sketching buildings, but not for construction."

"Oh, but he did design at least one building, his villa at Twickenham," said Edward, quick to support his hero.

"Nevertheless," continued Rhoda, "despite very distant origins both men became sought after by the owners of grand houses and we can picture some of those having Gillow furniture in their salons and Turner pictures on the walls. I wonder if they knew of each other?"

"I think they were probably somewhat different in character," added Edward. "Although neither came from initially 'important' families, Turner began life in difficult circumstances and seemed to be somewhat at odds with the art establishment for a while. I believe from what you say that Richard Gillow entered a well-established company and a family already known to rich patrons through his grandfather's and father's success. Moreover, the Gillows had social entry as practising Catholics to some northern county families of that persuasion but Turner had none, unless the clients of his father's wig-making business noticed him. Perhaps they did, because it was a habit at the time for hairdressers to display paintings and things in their shops, and the Turner shop was close to some small schools of art."

"Also in marked contrast," smiled Rhoda, "Richard Gillow II married the daughter of landed gentry and they had fourteen children, but Turner never married."

Rhoda and Edward were quite pleased to note that social mobility, though very rare, was not unknown in the eighteenth century and they recognised that of the two men in their conversation, it was the one from the lowest start who reached the highest acclaim.

If they shared that sympathy in a very small way, could it have been that whilst Edward came from a very ordinary background in what was then Lancashire, now a part of Cumbria, Rhoda had a slightly more privileged start in Essex?

Neither took their relative comfort now for granted.

What did intrigue Rhoda was the undoubted fact that she, as a southerner, was strongly attracted to the elegant products of a northern city while Edward, born in the north, found his enthusiasm in the art of a London man. She reflected that whereas hers was interest in the art of designers and workmen collaborating, his was in the output of one man. Hers was in the combination of beauty and use, his was in the joy of looking at objects without utility.

PART 3

Time honoured Lancaster
William Shakespeare. Richard II

CHAPTER 12

Unpacking necessities soon began when the travellers were ensconced in a rather comfortable hotel on the Lancaster University campus just off the M6 motorway near the city. Rhoda quietly prided herself that she had persuaded Edward to book in here because she had become aware of the fact that one of those rare microfilm copies of the Gillow company archives was housed in the university library and she had been able to get permission to view it. In any case she had once heard the campus described as reminiscent of an Italian hill town and she wanted to see it.

"Phew, the M6 was crowded," said Edward. "I vote we don't try to do anything else today after that journey. In any case it's getting dark. We should perhaps explore Lancaster tomorrow and spend time on the campus for your library work, the following day."

***

The day dawned a little blustery though fine and a few glimpses of sun; in short an ideal day for exploring a northern city on foot. Breakfast completed, they soon drove the couple of miles into the city centre and found a place to park very near to the castle. The enormous so-called John of Gaunt gateway beckoned from its prominent position high above the city.

"I've again been doing a bit of homework," Edward

slipped in, "the Gatehouse wasn't built until quite a time after John of Gaunt died. In any case there is little evidence that he spent much time in Lancaster, perhaps he preferred his birthplace Ghent. There is a tradition that the duke's horse shed a shoe in the centre of the city at what is now called 'Horseshoe Corner' where the (that is *a*) shoe is still visible, embedded in the road surface! I'd like to see that.

"Not much changes in central Lancaster, I'm glad to see. Fortunately the affluence of the 60s seems to have largely passed it by, so it escaped much of the demolition and rather tawdry development characteristic of that decade. Few cities can have retained so much of their Georgian and Victorian character. Even the mills, having lost their purpose, as well as chimneys, are now offering excellent student accommodation."

So ended for the moment Edward's tendency to quote the guidebooks to Rhoda on their travels.

Inside the castle courtyard they viewed the twelfth-century keep and the Well Tower where it was said the sixteenth century Pendle witches were incarcerated after being marched on foot the thirty miles from their homes in East Lancashire. They both found great interest in the old courtroom where malefactors were branded "M" on the palm with a still visible iron in the prisoners' dock. Rhoda could hardly suppress a shudder as she thought of how barbaric those times were. Even Edward found it disturbing when they were both locked in a dungeon cell by the guide to give them a feel for those days. He could only feel relieved that the work of a modern solicitor had not brought him into contact with such people.

"Let's get out into daylight," said Rhoda forcefully. "I simply can't imagine those poor souls subjected to that."

***

A few minutes later Edward who was slightly ahead called:

"Look at this view across Morecambe Bay to the Lake District Fells. You know Turner crossed those eight miles of tidal mud at least twice and painted two scenes of the coach and foot travellers arriving."

Back in his element, Edward was already remembering having seen one of those views engraved by Brandard for inclusion in the 1828 *Picturesque Views in England and Wales*. Secretly he felt sad that the boundary review of the 70s had thought it appropriate to 'steal' the best part of Lancashire across the bay and give it to the new county of Cumbria. Easy to forget though that most of the North West of England and some of Scotland was once called Cumbria. Even so it wasn't really clear to him that his birthplace could now be better administered from Carlisle on the other side of England's greatest mountains, than from Lancaster. The passing of the once practical trade route across the bay might one day be corrected if the proposed barrage was ever built with a road, he mused.

Rhoda was turning to her right but managed to say:

"It's wonderful, love," as she became distracted by the sight of the Priory Church ahead of her and standing next to the castle. They must at least pop their heads into such a beautiful building.

They were soon both entranced by the choir stalls. All the more so with accompaniment of fine organ playing. Rhoda couldn't remember having ever seen such luxuriant canopies. A churchwarden told her that they were said to have been moved to the priory from Furness or Cockersand Abbey.

Edward was pouring over his guidebook.

"If we retreat down the big steps between church and castle we should find a narrow little street down to the oldest house in the city. It is called 'The Judges' Lodgings' because after being the house of the keepers of the castle for a couple of centuries, it was furnished by *guess who* to welcome their lordships presiding at the castle courtroom."

Rhoda had been doing some reading as well and pointed out that they would then find themselves immediately next to the original Gillow workshop at the bottom.

She tried not to sound too excited as they made the descent to the house and began a tour.

***

"This house is splendid and a great place for this beautiful furniture," she breathed. "Even judges must have felt intimidated by such finery, don't you think?"

As a man who had experienced his own share of being intimidated *by* judges, Edward could only think that it would be a good thing if it might have put them in the right mood to listen to sensible lawyers like himself.

Rhoda really liked a display of apprentices' work and tools but most admired the pièces de résistances; the Chippendale-style desk made for Sir James Ibbetson in 1778 which had remained in his family ever since, and the absolutely beautiful inlaid bookcase of the same period once owned by the wife of a wealthy West Indies merchant in Lancaster. Since Ibbetson lived near Ilkley and therefore well acquainted with the origin of the Chippendales at Otley, it is something of a tribute to the workmanship of the Gillow men that he allowed it to be made in Lancaster, though he did argue at the price and was simply told that if he wanted the best, he would need to pay for the best! Chippendale senior died in the year the desk was made but Ibbetson could easily have commissioned Chippendale junior in London to make his father's design for him.

***

Of course Edward had no intention of spoiling Rhoda's new-found enthusiasm for this treasure house of wonderful objects, but secretly he could hardly wait to travel on towards his prime objective on the Pennine hills fifty miles north.

"There is a lot to see in this city isn't there?" he ventured. "You know Turner stayed here and painted views of the city from the hill to the east. Another of his drawings shows the river and the magnificent aqueduct bridge which was built less than twenty years before he visited. It would be quite hard to imagine the sailing ships coming in on that river to the centre of the city if it were not for the survival of the quayside warehouses and the customs house."

Rhoda quickly pointed out that this last building was designed by Richard Gillow and built in 1764. Like other men of his time it was not unusual to be both architect and furniture designer. "Perhaps his love of the Palladian style we can see in that building was reflected in the clean and well-proportioned lines of his furniture," she thought. At least it facilitated import of the fine timbers required for his work and export of some of the products.

Whilst in the city there was just time remaining to fulfil Edward's plan of buying suitable clothing for the next phase of the holiday. He normally boasted about his antipathy to shopping, but almost enjoyed the task of finding good anoraks under what he considered to be expert advice.

CHAPTER 13

They thought the views across Morecambe Bay from the university campus spectacular, but appreciated the shelter given by the layout of the buildings grouped around small squares and interconnected by a covered walkway.

"There are two library buildings on the campus plan, Edward. This is the main one opening off the central large square and in front of it is an interesting smaller one exclusively housing the Ruskin archive brought from the Isle of Wight. The building is a masterpiece of Sir Richard MacCormac, I'm told. It has academic links to the Ruskin collection in his house on Coniston Lake. Why don't you ask if you could spend time in that library? He wrote a lot about your beloved Turner so you may be able to see something of that connection."

"Yes, their lives overlapped by about thirty years and they knew each other for about ten years," Edward remembered.

Indeed Edward did spend time there and enjoyed sitting in the peace and quiet of the reading room at a wonderful table and chairs commissioned from a first class furniture designer and maker on the edge of the Lake District National Park. It was good to see local tradition alive and well. He found books by Ruskin which he didn't know existed and absorbed himself in teasing out the great man's comments on Turner. One small disappointment for him his discovery that Ruskin considered Turner to be more interested in convex rather than concave shapes in mountain scenery. Thinking about this made him wonder for a moment whether Turner might have abandoned painting High Cup Nick because of the hollow of the U-shaped valley below.

As Rhoda went off to see the Gillow archives and expected to be delayed by them, she called, "We can meet back in the hotel." It was only a couple of hundred yards away.

**

Both were happy to pursue their interests alone for a while, albeit amid the hustle and bustle of life on a residential, collegiate campus. It pleased them to see so many young people from so many diverse backgrounds, going about their business and chatting. They were impressed to recall that such a relatively new university had already made its mark amongst the older traditional ones.

The Gillow archive copies turned out to be microfilm of scores of notebooks of the company dating from 1731 to 1895. Rhoda was shown how to work the film reader and was allowed to see the pages of the estimate sketchbook which contained details of a portable desk similar to hers.

Her fingers were trembling as she turned to the relevant pages. After something of a struggle requiring a lot of patience, with a sharp intake of breath, she recognised a drawing exactly like her desk and showing the same measurements. On the opposite page were the details and costs of each piece of wood and fittings. She could barely resist a shout of triumph as she read the name of the journeyman who had made it and been paid thirteen shillings. He was W. Naylor, the name pencilled on the drawer of her desk! She was convinced that her desk must be one of two which he had made in October 1792.

Elsewhere in the library she found that W. Naylor was employed by Gillows for many years and had made many pieces for the firm, including a coffin for one of his own relations who had died in 1786. Rhoda thought she remembered that Hepplewhite had died in that year also.

Back at the hotel Edward drily said, on hearing some of this, that clearly Naylor had been promoted from making one kind of box to another. More seriously he wondered if his family had been joiners for generations with a name like his.

"He must have worked jolly hard," said Rhoda. "He made a couple of dining tables, several bookcases, a sideboard, a wardrobe and many more pieces the year he made my desk."

***

The next day they were ready to head north to Edward's main objective.

"If we join the motorway a couple of miles south of here and then turn north," explained Edward, "we could bypass the city."

"Yes," agreed Rhoda, "that would give us time to leave the motorway at Carnforth from where Leighton Hall can be easily reached in ten minutes."

Edward quickly realised that he would have to postpone his wishes until Rhoda had seen the Gillow family home.

"Actually I'm really enjoying this shared adventure, dear. This trip is as much yours as mine and I've secretly been fascinated by your enthusiasm for these Gillow people. In any case we are nearly back in my neck of the woods when I was a boy, so I'm really enjoying these diversions."

Neither of them were quite ready for the view of the hall down its magnificent driveway with the Lakeland mountains visible as backcloth peeping out over Arnside Knott.

"You go in the house, Rhoda, I'm going to take a walk up the hill over there. The chap at the gatehouse told me the view from there is right across the bay and includes the mountains. I think I can see a seat at the top and we can meet there if you wish to climb the grassy slope to join me later. It does look pretty steep, but maybe that will help to get us in shape for High Cup Nick."

It was a short though steep ascent but the view was so rewarding. Not only from up here did the house look like a miniature mansion nestling in the basin of its green park but the view beyond certainly was spectacular from Edward's elevated position.

After a while the tiny figure of Rhoda emerged from the house and slowly began the ascent. She arrived somewhat out of breath and needed a few minutes to recover.

"The man was absolutely right, Rhoda. Turn round and feast your eyes as soon as you've got your breath back." Seated together they exchanged experiences as they munched chocolate bars. Edward spoke first as he spread his arms wide to embrace the scene. From somewhere he had produced his map and identified many of the sights.

"Behind the house is Leighton Moss the well-known RSPB reserve. You know I have read that there are bitterns in those reeds with their distinctive booming. Beyond is Arnside Knott and then in the distance the mountains. It was a favourite haunt of local man Eric Morecambe, a very keen bird watcher as well as being such a funny man."

Rhoda could see, as she had done up at Lancaster Castle,

that Edward kept allowing his gaze to swing to the west across the vast expanse of the bay. She knew why. Across there was Barrow-in-Furness, a few miles west of his birthplace at Dendron. Having taken his name, she felt herself just a little connected with the region. He reminded her too that Turner himself had crossed that vast expanse in his 1816 tour. Not from Barrow, of course. It hardly existed then when the principal town on that side of the bay was Ulverston.

"The birthplace of another very funny man," Edward remarked.

"Who was that?"

"Why, Stan Laurel of Laurel and Hardy was born there."

"Funny how so many great comedians came from the North," added Rhoda.

"Still do," commented Edward. "If you didn't have a sense of humour you wouldn't last long. From where we are standing we can see where Laurel as a youngster, Eric Morecambe, Victoria Wood and Thora Hird observed human behaviour with acute sensitivity. Perhaps they took themselves much less seriously than most of us tend to do these days."

Edward couldn't take his eyes off the scene in front of him as he reflected on the close association of these people with the sands of the bay whilst he tried to imagine it as a thoroughfare with Turner crossing.

"I wonder if we will see a party of tourists making their way with their guide, perhaps feeling similar nostalgia as I am. Someone told me just yesterday that the present guide, one of a line twenty-five long appointed by the monarch since 1548, is about to retire having trained his successor. My local informant was quite chatty and enthusiastically remarked that although serving for fifty years he couldn't claim to have conducted Turner across, but he did safely guide the consort of the present monarch. I wish I had done the walk when I was a teenager. I reckon I still could do the eight or so miles without too much effort as long as the guide keeps me out of the notorious quicksands and dangerous channels. In our present period of political uncertainty, it's wonderful to hear of such dedicated leadership with immense trust shown by his followers."

After those thoughts Edward had to bring himself up with a start to listen to Rhoda's account of her experience.

"I've had such a rewarding visit, Edward. The lady of the house insisted on showing me round herself. She was so nice. Not in the least pretentious. It is clear that the house with its wonderful furniture is very much still a family home. You should see the fine expanding dining table; an example of their Imperial table invented about 1804 and now to be seen in many great houses. Funnily enough, the Gillow family didn't have one of their own when they came to furnish their 'new' mansion down there and had to buy it back from a customer! It is served by six much older chairs which I was told were probably made for the founder of the company in the 1750s or 60s. And as an afterthought," she added. "You would have liked the Guardi in the passageway, I'm sure."

"Yes I would," said a slightly disappointed Edward. "I've always preferred his scenes of Venice to Canaletto! They seem to me to capture so much of the atmosphere of the place rather than meticulous architectural drawings for the wealthy Grand Tour customers." He liked to be a bit controversial about such questions especially when there was no one there to contradict him.

Rhoda preferred to change the subject rather than

challenge him.

"Did you bring that flask out of the car? This is such a wonderful place to enjoy morning coffee. Then we must move on towards your goal."

"I've been waiting for this opportunity for some time, as you know, love," began Edward, "but to be honest I really haven't got a clue how we might proceed. Of course I am looking forward to seeing the subject of these sketches and that in itself will make a rewarding holiday, but I keep wondering how to set about trying to discover if a painting does exist. We can hardly knock on doors to ask if someone secretly has it on their wall!"

At least Edward could see the funny side of his wishes. Rhoda simply hoped that he wouldn't be too disappointed if he made no progress at all, which is what she expected to happen. They both put these thoughts out of their minds as they started the next phase of their journey, trying not to liken it to the Grand Tour of their predecessors on art and culture hunts. They didn't want to get anything totally out of proportion.

PART 4

"Places where a man may be humbled"
A. H. Griffin

CHAPTER 14

The uneventful journey to Appleby later that day started on the M6 motorway. Neither of them particularly liked motorways but this one on the stretch from Lancaster to their turning at Tebay offered views again of the Lakeland mountains to the west. Fortunately it carried less traffic load than further south. Then they enjoyed the very scenic stretch through the Lune Gorge beneath the Howgill hills.

"I'd no idea that we had such a dramatic route," enthused Rhoda who tended to think motorways boring.

"I thought I would surprise you," said Edward from behind the wheel. "I checked the map to see how the road builders had dealt with this stretch. Then I realised that the River Lune had cut its way between these mountain ranges which allowed the railway surveyors to get through, so why not follow their route? I like the look of that Howgill range above us on the right, don't you? They look tranquil on a day like this and perhaps are quieter than some of the Lakeland peaks have become after Wainwright popularised them. By all accounts he'd be the last person to want to see them crowded but happy to know that so many now appreciated their beauty and character. In that, he probably had an even greater influence than Wordsworth or Beatrix Potter."

"Let's give them equal credit," protested Rhoda who had been brought up on Peter Rabbit and soon graduated to admiring Wordsworth, whereas until now she had never heard of Alfred Wainwright.

Rhoda quite liked being the navigator and shortly warned Edward that their turning off the motorway was imminent. She enjoyed the next stretch over the moorland between Orton and Appleby. They were delighted but needed to take care as they encountered sheep taking charge of the unfenced road.

"We must stop and look back south," exclaimed Edward. He had recognised the place as near where Turner had stopped to sketch the view south where he was destined to ride towards his next commission. They looked down on that gap between the Lake District mountains and the Howgill fells, where the River Lune took its course towards the sea. Before railway or motorway surveyors had settled on this route, Turner himself had ridden it. This was getting even better by the moment.

Rhoda could already feel anticipation of arrival at the region of Edward's intended exploration. After all she had been the one to benefit most so far from their holiday. Now her obsession could be put on one side whilst Edward pursued his. They were both happy to support each other in a holiday with such clear intentions and so far the weather forecasters had been on their side.

***

Another comfortable hotel welcomed them in the centre of Appleby.

"I'm pleased you booked us in here. It's so well placed for us to explore the town and promises to be very comfortable. I can't wait to walk out of the front door and look up this magnificent street towards the castle up the hill, and the church just below us."

"Well there's nothing to stop us right now," came from Edward in the bathroom who thought unpacking, indeed packing for that matter, should be a task of minutes rather than hours.

"At least let us have a pot of tea in that attractive entrance hall where we can watch the world go by, or anyway the bits of it that choose to pop in here for quick refreshment during a tour of the town. Perhaps we might meet some locals who may be able to point us in interesting directions," shouted Rhoda from practically within the handsome clothes press where she was hanging the town clothes from her suitcase.

Her new anorak from a Lancaster shop was already hooked on the back of the door until needed for exploration. True to character, Edward hadn't brought a lot more than his driving clothes and a few shirts and things, except for the all-important boots, over-trousers just in case and his trusty waterproof jacket with years of good wear. The notion of changing it for fashion and colour when it wasn't worn out was anathema to a man who had grown up within sight of the Lakeland mountains. What was wrong with re-proofing a jacket with Nikwax and the satisfaction of a job well done as droplets formed and ran off and left him protected? But he did admire Rhoda's taste in holiday clothing, understated but most attractive, yet serviceable. He hoped it left for discussion only what was suitable for dinner that evening and he had brought a decent jumper and even a lightweight jacket neither of which would make him stand out, he thought, and certainly not put Rhoda in the shade. He just hoped it wouldn't embarrass her either. Despite his bluster he quietly admitted to himself that her mantra of 'being well dressed is to be suitably dressed' was absolutely right. But did he need a tie? He decided he would wear one for the first foray into the dining room. He had reluctantly brought one.

His thoughts were suddenly interrupted as Rhoda announced that she was ready to go down for a cuppa hoping to get Yorkshire tea with perhaps a sprinkling of Earl Grey, and a piece of fruitcake. Within minutes they were feeling rested after an interesting but tiring drive and ready to talk about the next few days.

"I know you don't like too much planning when we are on holiday," volunteered Edward, "but I've been looking at the local forecast and it will be rather overcast tomorrow, but clearer, even sunny on Wednesday. Suppose we explore Appleby tomorrow and walk up to High Cup Nick on Wednesday. From what the boys said, High Cup is so much more revealing in decent weather because the views can be so long. We can look round down here as long as it isn't actually raining."

"OK," said Rhoda. "We need to do a bit more homework to make sure we can find the places described in that old guidebook of the town you just spotted in a second-hand shop across the road while I was parking the car."

"I can't believe that it was apparently written by a young man who holidayed in this town decades ago," said Edward. "Still, history of a town like this doesn't change overnight."

"Well it was," Rhoda confirmed. "I've got it here. Somebody wrote it in the 1950s. I wonder where he is now?"

Bending over a silver teapot and a newspaper across the room was an elderly but still extremely healthy looking man in a tweed jacket, who quietly, but courteously intervened at this point.

"I wonder if you would mind if I joined you for a few

minutes, I assure you, just a few. You see, I wrote that guide when I was a teenager on family holidays."

Edward and Rhoda were stunned at this coincidence.

"Not so much of a coincidence," said their new acquaintance. "I retired to the next town and often come back here to enjoy the place where I spent some time as a youth. May I point you to just a few of Appleby's gems, without, I hope, spoiling your enjoyment of them by saying too much? There is no substitute for personal exploration, is there? First let me say there are more modern guidebooks available, some perhaps written by more modern people!" He neglected to say that one of them was his recent update of the one in their hands. If the travellers needed any encouragement to explore the erstwhile county town of Westmorland, in that few minutes they were spellbound to hear what they might see on the morrow. It was explained how much influence Lady Anne Clifford had on the town and its buildings and how the character of the town changed on opposite sides of the river. Curiously the oldest part on the east bank now superficially looked the more recent part because it had been more developed whilst the 'newer' part on the hill of the west bank overtook it in the second half of the seventeenth century, largely under the influence of Lady Anne.

"Thank you so much," they said almost in unison as their advisor finished. "It is one thing to read history, but quite another to hear it from someone with so much local knowledge and feeling for this town and area."

They immediately felt that this part of their holiday was off to a very good start. Of course, their informant had no knowledge of Edward's pipe dream but his friendliness led them to believe that if local people had means of helping, however unknowingly, they would.

95

CHAPTER 15

As Edward and Rhoda wandered around Appleby they became more and more absorbed in its history and architecture. Perhaps more obviously than most towns its modern character seemed to have developed as its history unfolded. They clearly felt that the castle on top of the hill dominated the town, whilst the church nestled by the river below. That made them feel a little uncomfortable at first because they were more used to towns in which the church was the most prominent building and usually the oldest surviving one, indicative of the power of the establishment over the people at the time. In between the two on the sides of the steeply sloping street were the merchants' houses and public buildings including where they were staying. Rhoda pointed out with guidebook in hand that in reality castle and church were closely linked, in that Lady Anne Clifford from the castle had had a good deal to do with the present appearance of parts of the church.

"She must have been an extraordinary woman," enthused Rhoda, "to have broken through the glass ceiling of her time much as she effortlessly broke through walls of castles, if she needed more stone for her enterprises. What other woman of her time would have caused a monument to her family, and later her own tomb to be erected in this church, before she died?"

That formidable lady even though then in her seventh decade and even though she owned castles in Brough,

Brougham and Pendragon nearby, as well as Skipton and Bardon in Yorkshire had huge influence on Appleby. Her great progressions along the flank of Mallerstang valley with full entourage of up to 300 must have been a terrific, even terrifying sight to behold as she caused her castles to be restored for her use without losing energy for restoring several churches as well, including two in Appleby. It is said that she travelled in a horse-litter with ladies-in-waiting in a coach. Then followed many men-servants, carts and horses, even furniture; a retinue probably not matched until the Duke of Windsor crossed the Atlantic with trunks and cars and sufficient followers to occupy half the state cabins in the *Queen Mary*.

Rhoda and Edward couldn't help thinking of Anne in the same way as Bess of Hardwick had seemed to them when they had visited Hardwick Hall. As a favourite of Elizabeth's court, it might not have been expected that Anne would turn her back on metropolitan life and choose to restore her neglected estates in the North.

***

Being closest to their hotel it was unsurprising that they chose to visit the church first. They were confronted by Anne Clifford's family monument which captured Rhoda's imagination.

Meanwhile Edward was closely examining the fine, very old organ case which he read had come from Carlisle cathedral. They were both delighted when they noticed that the organist was just about to strike up and they sat to hear his beautiful rendering of Widor's Toccata and Fugue.

It wasn't at all difficult for them to imagine a traveller like Turner staying in or at least visiting this town. They felt strongly that he would have seen much of what they were enjoying. Did he feel uplifted in the same way by its history and people they asked themselves, or only by its architecture?

"Somehow it seems so arrogant to try to put oneself into the mind of a genius," thought Edward aloud, "but if we are to try to find if a painting ever existed, this seems to be the time and place to do so."

Their discovery that the almshouses just below the castle entrance were founded by Lady Anne encouraged them to divert briefly into the pretty courtyard where they were delighted to chat to one or two of the current residents. A particularly nice old lady welcomed them to Appleby as if they were old friends and showed them the tiny chapel in which she and her friends worshipped. She explained that they held their own tradition that Turner the artist had visited here 200 years before the Dendrons, on his way up to the castle to which he had been summoned by Lord Thanet. Such rumours could easily have reached their predecessors many of whom were retired servants from the castle.

"That really was a very worthwhile stop," said Edward as they regained the street. "Do you realise that we have just heard the first suggestion that Turner may not only have been here, but could have had an invitation up to the castle. I suppose he was quite famous by then, and certainly well known to landowners further south in Yorkshire."

"Yes," added Rhoda. "He was a remarkable traveller wasn't he, considering that a mere eleven years after his death visitors would have been arriving in Appleby by train, a complete revolution of travel in England? I wonder if that technology would have made him less likely to visit High Cup Nick in the manner of some car travellers now who see the countryside only from the viewpoints of roads."

"With that thought I'm determined that we should leave ours in the valley tomorrow and get up there under our own steam, so to speak," proposed Edward. He knew that it was their only option if they wished to stand where he believed Turner had stood before them.

Time remained today for them to complete their ascent of this wonderful street to the castle and join a small party to be conducted around by its present owner. There was no mention of Turner or his paintings on the tour.

***

Turning their backs on the castle gateway as they emerged, the view was across the town to the spreading ridge of the northern Pennine hills as they march north-west to their highest point. Despite a long plateau as its summit, Cross Fell reached within seventy feet of the magical three thousand. To its right could be seen the somewhat more prominent, though slightly lower, Dun Fells. Edward rather felt that the wilderness the mountains represented was now somewhat compromised by the white spheres of the radar station on the higher of these two. He didn't think he could quite see High Cup Nick even further east but he could see the challenge of gaining two thirds of this height tomorrow on the way to their objective. He didn't like to draw Rhoda's attention too much to the hills, on his principle that they always look more challenging from a distance than when actually under foot. At least he convinced himself of that and hoped that she would agree, next day.

CHAPTER 16

Edward loved pouring over printed maps even though he had invested in a GPS for safety reasons. He could spend hours in Stanford's of Covent Garden. Once a compass had been his constant companion and he still carried it in his backpack.

"One of the glories as well as the downside of High Cup Nick is that there isn't a road, the nearest being about a four-mile hike from it so we are in for an eight-mile round trip on foot by the shortest possible route. It's nearly 500 metres up and we shouldn't be disturbed by anyone who isn't prepared to countenance that."

"Well I'm game," came from Rhoda. "That's why we are here."

Edward chipped in:

"It's only about eight miles to Dufton from here on rather narrow roads, I'm told. Just so long as we don't meet too many of those huge John Deere tractors. We can strike up from there on the track now forming part of the Pennine Way. According to my map it's actually a diversion for hikers doing the Way because there isn't any other accommodation between Langdon Beck and Garrigill, a distance of at least twenty miles along the Pennine ridge. We need to make a prompt start to comfortably cover our more realistic eight miles. We are lucky with the weather. The manager here says the forecast is good for a day or two and there won't be too much wind or rain. We should get good views from the top."

Rhoda was happy with that as long as time was made to get a pie each to go with the flask she had made up in the bedroom. Anoraks were already stowed in their backpack and their fleeces would keep them warm if the energetic walking didn't. Both had good footwear.

Half an hour later they were parking in Dufton.

"This is a very attractive village," said Rhoda. "I do hope that we shall have time on our return to walk around and explore it. I love the rich colour of the red sandstone round here. It really gives a special character to these buildings grouped around the village green."

Edward responded:

"We will see half of it as we walk back along the road to the start of the track and I understand that the pub is in the other direction from the car so we should see most of the rest of the village on our return. I propose that we eat at the pub this evening. It's now called The Stag but our host in Appleby explained that it was once The Buck. At least the re-naming makes complete sense and they weren't tempted to call it the Slug and Lettuce in those days!"

***

The track began as a fairly good farm lane, a bit muddy and stony in places with even a stream crossing but not large enough to need a bridge, at least today. But it was easy to imagine a swollen torrent so close to the hills. Even some of the tarmac roads around here crossed rivers at a ford.

Ascent would have been found fairly gradual to more seasoned walkers or perhaps to Rhoda and Edward a decade or two ago. But they had tried to keep themselves in decent shape with weekend rambles and the occasional walking holiday. When they were younger they had enjoyed those kind of packages in which small but welcoming family-run hotels provide excellent bases to which to return each evening. They preferred unguided but clearly described day treks with local maps and where necessary passes to public transport. It gave a degree of freedom followed by good company and much anticipated local dishes. Best of all they liked those in Europe with mountain scenery and ski lifts to the alpine meadows in summer. Those memories were put aside in favour of much harsher landscape as they climbed today. The feeling of freedom though was even greater when they began to realise how vast the spaces in the Pennines are. Claims issued to the media from Whitehall of more than forty per cent of England being available space in the context of provision of new towns, whilst perhaps strictly true, omit to mention that much is over a thousand feet above sea level. It isn't habitable even by hardy upland folks. It can be easy to walk all day and not see another soul.

Edward still liked to think in terms of feet rather than metres because he could judge more exactly what was ahead using his youthful experience. He did admit to himself that he found the sound of one thousand feet more satisfactory to conquer than a mere 330 metres.

Within half a mile of leaving Dufton by the farm track, the explorers began to see on their left a most remarkable hill, some would call mountain, rising straight out of the farmland and forming almost a pyramid shape which Rhoda thought might be similar in size to the great pyramid of Gizeh. In actual fact it was roughly twice the height of Cheops' building. It wasn't their objective but Edward gave himself a promise to return and conquer it. He had seen it on his map named Dufton Pike.

Instead they pressed on climbing a section of the famous Pennine Way. A couple more miles taken more easily than they expected were accompanied by a raising of their spirits as they sensed rather than clearly saw the beginnings of a huge depression to their right. The track was now more of a rough and uneven path no longer gaining so much new height as traversing smaller rocky depressions sometimes with tumbling becks crossing. These were once or twice bridged with stone slabs, or occasionally to be forded with a modicum of hopping from rock to rock offering natural stepping stones and perhaps the exciting safe risk of wet boots or sopping socks if tackled badly.

"Hold on, dear," came from Rhoda, "I can't really quite keep up this pace. Don't you think this might be a good spot for a bit of a break? You know, a bit of re-charging."

Edward began dragging out stuff from his backpack and triumphantly emerged with a bag containing two Cornish pasties bought whilst Rhoda was busy elsewhere in the shops of Appleby that morning. There were apples and a banana as well as chocolate biscuits all to be washed down with coffee or juice to compliment the obligatory water bottles. In truth, Edward really preferred his concoction of peanut butter and Marmite on a sandwich when hiking, but had been unable to find the yeast extract in Appleby.

Rhoda had chosen the spot well. Here were rocks offering dry seating and both were looking forward to a rough and ready lunch. There is no better way of re-fuelling on a mountain hike than this, they thought. So far they had not seen another traveller and this novelty seemed to them to give the freedom which these hills beckoned.

**

In the next half mile the canyon to the right was revealing a rim of dramatic vertical cliffs giving way below to an enormous U-shaped valley of great symmetry. Soon, from its head they at last stood at the Nick itself debouching down a rocky and very rough scree into the greener valley beneath their feet, itself stretching for more than a mile to the farmlands below. There was no hyperbole whatsoever in describing it to each other as 'awesome' – an expression they usually tried to avoid, not least because of its prominence in the vocabulary of American tourists.

Despite being completely in the mountains now, they were delighted to see almost verdant small patches of nutritious grass. On these were congregated small groups of sheep who sought them out among the rushes and coarser vegetation. A little above them was heather moor with bilberry from which they could hear grouse calling in their cheerful *kowk, ok-ok-ok* way, being unable to forecast the impending 'glorious' twelfth.

"I don't know whether I am more concerned with the thought of wild grouse being shot for sport, or the rearing of pheasants and partridge just to be blasted into pieces," thought Rhoda.

Any weariness in their limbs disappeared in the face of a spectacular view down to the Eden Valley a thousand feet below and beyond. If the Eden Valley deserves its name as it rightly does, this spot overlooking it gives an impressive vision of paradise. Our intrepid hikers could hardly speak, not from their exertions but rather from merely standing still in this literally breathtaking situation poised between mountain desolation and the handiwork of massive glaciation gouging out the softer rocks below to leave bastions of basalt columns at the edge. Projecting from them was a needle of rock to become known as Nicholas' Tower after the local shoemaker of that name who was said in local lore to have climbed it and fashioned a pair of boots on its tiny summit.

***

For a couple who had so recently been admiring the greens of a beautiful southern woodland, to see the dominant browns of a high moorland as equally dramatic and attractive perhaps required some mental adjustment. They were helped in this by the appearance of another hiker who addressed them in the manner familiar to frequent fell walkers.

"Hi, have you come up from Dufton or across the moor?"

No answer was really required. It was simply a way of opening a (short) conversation and ensuring that all was well without the need to ask. But Edward did say how much he was taken by the feeling of isolation and peace in this spectacularly coloured landscape.

"We are very privileged to be here by our own efforts aren't we?" the walker said. "For similar colours and atmosphere you should see the paintings by the Grasmere artist Heaton Cooper who captured them so well especially as the sun begins to set."

As the man went on his way, Edward made a mental note to visit the Cooper gallery in that Lakeland village. For now he was intent on drinking in Turner's supposed view across the huge sweep of landscape with evidence in the foreground of how it might have been formed.

"Which way would Turner have come to get here, Edward?" mused Rhoda.

"From the east," he said. "Apparently there has been for a long time a bridleway across from the River Tees. It is now more or less followed by the Pennine Way and crosses the Tees just to the south of where the chemical giant ICI built a reservoir to supply their huge factory complex at Billingham near Middlesborough. By any standards it must have been terrible terrain and you have to respect someone who would tackle that in the name of art. I think even mountain bikers might find this ground challenging. We are here in quite good weather fortunately, but imagine how it would be when he struck a bad patch."

Rhoda's thoughts of the comfort to come in the valley were already uppermost and she tried not to imagine it. But Edward did, because he had read that the summer of 1816 was the worst experienced in England, perhaps a result of major volcanic activity on the other side of the world the year before. He knew that crops had almost failed.

***

Behind them was a plateau of boggy mountainside lying at nearly two thousand feet between hills rising even more to the east and west. Edward and Rhoda were elated to have climbed to this altitude from the village below. It was across this plateau that travellers approached this place from the reaches of the valley of the Tees to the east. Edward tried to imagine an artist coming that way 200 years ago. It would then, as now, have been treeless; near the height beyond which trees could establish even if there were no wind or sheep. It almost beggars belief that a southern city dweller of that time could have made such a journey alone. Edward had to force himself to recollect the purpose of being here.

He could recall the sketches fairly clearly. What was a mystery to him was how Turner could have stood at this spot and sketched without the full intention of completing a painting. No. He couldn't have done. There must be a painting somewhere. Would it ever be found?

"It is good at this end of the day that going down will be less arduous than coming up," affirmed Rhoda.

"On this route that's true," came the thoughtful response, "but I remember that in my youthful walking days I realised that a steep descent could be harder on the body, especially knees, than going up and particularly when more tired."

If the thought of returning the four miles to Dufton might have seemed formidable, the sheer pleasure of their experience obscured any concern until almost without realising it they found themselves approaching civilisation again. The fact that they both had very good footwear in the form of proper walking boots had made it a relatively comfortable day with none of the rough ground presenting too many challenges. And they were facing down towards the paradise valley.

Despite the lure of anticipated comforts, they were both feeling elated with an energetic but hugely rewarding day. Edward could not help recalling the words of a hymn he used to sing at school assembly. 'Hills of the North rejoice; river and mountain spring.' He needed to explain to Rhoda why his foot was tapping out Martin Shaw's tune on the gravel path.

"How fortunate are those who can access these hills

regularly," considered Edward who was becoming quietly envious of those who could. To him this was the real England, away from the busy and sometimes noisy world, though he knew that those who were the true inhabitants here could have a hard time making a living. Their great strength, he mused, not in a paternalistic way, was finding their reward in the countryside itself and the friendships forged there.

"Snap out of it Edward, dear. We are nearly back to the real world."

***

The Stag Inn beckoned from its prominent though discrete frontage onto the expansive central green of this exquisite place.

"How tempting," he sighed as they entered Dufton again.

"That fountain on the edge of the green is very unusual, isn't it?" exclaimed Rhoda who was carefully trying to make out the inscription around the top.

"Oh it's in Latin. I don't think my O-level swotting is anywhere near up to that. It seems to be something about a clear pool and shepherds. Well it is hardly relevant now that its trough is full of soil and nice flowers. Turner wouldn't have seen it. It wasn't built then according to this notice."

Sure enough, across the green was the Stag Inn, fronting onto the grass and projecting its welcome even across to where they stood. When they reached the threshold, the friendliness even extended to muddy boots if necessary.

CHAPTER 17

After a feast of Swaledale lamb and a taste of local ale, Edward and Rhoda were in the mood to open up conversation with one or two locals at the bar of this welcoming, unpretentious old hostelry.

When scouting around at the south end of the village they had realised that if Turner had come down the main track south from High Cup Nick, he would have passed Dufton Hall and entered the village. Did he break his journey here, or head straight on to Appleby? Edward wondered whether to broach the subject with one of the locals. He chose a kind-looking middle-aged man on an adjacent bench. After a few pleasantries he broached the subject of Turner and his trips to the North to paint. Oh yes, the man had heard of Turner but he didn't know anything of a visit to these parts, perhaps unsurprisingly since he came from Leeds but had a static caravan on a nearby site. He and his wife agreed that Dufton was a superb base for hill walking. They often climbed Dufton Pike for the spectacular views in almost all directions to Cross Fell and the Dun Fells in the north to the distant Lake District mountains across the Eden valley. His advice was to talk to proper locals.

Over in the corner of the bar a couple of young chaps were quietly talking, recovering from an energetic day on tractor and harvester in the fields to the west beyond the village car park and before the hills rose steeply to the Pennine escarpment. Both were dressed in the working clothes of the country, not the tweeds so beloved of some of the incomers and visitors to the village. Not that they weren't welcome as long as they added to its community life and economy. Jobs were scarce now, and new residents as well as weekend walkers and campers were needed. One of them called Jason knew from his father that work had only been there by courtesy (the word oxymoron wasn't much used in these parts) of the landowners and mine proprietors. He considered that the landowners had looked after the landscape and in some cases helped to create it. More so than the mining bosses who had helped to tear it apart and left scars and derelict buildings.

Not for ever, though. Even the hushes gouged to expose mineral veins, and the industrial relics were being largely reclaimed by the wilderness which they had for a time despoiled. Not so permanent as some of the great towns and cities which they had helped to build. But they were known as relatively good employers being Quakers owning the London-based Lead Mining Company. For a time they had joined and indeed helped to form the 'northern power house' of its day.

***

These twenty-something young men enjoying a drink were far from being country yokels. Farming in the Eden Valley had always been profitable. On these more upland areas on the flanks of the valley, villages like Dufton ringing the lower slopes of the Pennine hills had in their hay-day (!) supported one or two gentry leaving behind houses of significant size and style. Then, life on the land and in the mines on the hills was extremely hard for the labourers and maybe some dreamt of the growing cities with their promises of work. They had perhaps not had the opportunity to read Mrs Gaskell's *North and South*, though Dufton had a small, but locally very influential reading room. It had helped to educate many since it was built along with the village school by those Quaker bosses opening up mining in the hills. Some of that income profited the village community.

Now, with mechanisation, work on these sometimes steeply sloping fields had become a little lighter and, after a tough day, these men were enjoying excellent draft bitter. They had time to discuss world affairs as well as the young beauty said to have moved into the next village, Murton. The village school had served them well and a few years in secondary in Appleby had rounded off an education making them both anxious to return to village life. They wanted to feel part of a community they had always known and to which they felt they could contribute.

Jason was son of a gentleman farmer who could send him to Appleby School and the other, Simon the brighter of the two went to agricultural college at Penrith after secondary school. But they had remained good friends since those junior days at the village 'academy' though Jason had inherited his father's farm and had become Simon's employer.

They were deep in conversation working out how to buy a bigger tractor and if it could be used on this land. The farm had to go to the expense and labour of widening gates from the traditional eight to ten feet for the last generation of machines, but now they knew it would need twelve-foot wide gaps. Then there was the question of the narrow country lanes in these parts.

***

"Let's have another pint," said Jason. "I've something important I want you to hear before we go home. You heard what that couple from south were talking about to the pair from Leeds. They were clearly interested in this Turner chap's visit to Dufton and what he did when he was here. I caught something about a High Cup painting, but then Jess's dog over there made a bit of a row, and I didn't catch the rest. You know I'm always up for a deal, Simon. But who was this Turner dude? I know I'm the educated one, but I spent a fair amount of my time on the rugger field and not much in the library beyond my formal studies. You were the curious one, not having quite such a privileged home and more determined than I was to make a way in the world by your own efforts. Tell me about him when we've had another pint. It's my round."

***

"Well, I see myself as a practical fellow, steeped more in solving farming problems than in book learning," replied Simon when his whistle was sufficiently wet.

"But I've always been keen on village life and history since Miss Truegood told us about it at junior school, so I've done a bit of time in the village reading room up by gaffer Ernest's cottage. I see Ernest there anyways sometimes for he can read and sure does after the morning paper comes."

"Ernest told me about this guy from London who came here two centuries ago to sketch. He reckoned the traveller had been around Yorkshire, Lancashire and Westmorland, when it was still called that officially and before county boundary people in offices took a chunk of Lancashire and giv' it to this new-fangled Cumbria together with Cumberland and Westmorland. This chap Turner would find himself lost if he tried his old maps to get himself across Morecambe Bay by the sands route from one part of Lancashire to the other. Westmorland folk still talk about their county even though Appleby is no longer the old historic county town. An orchestra in Kendal is still called Westmorland Symphonia, they tell me, though I've never heard it. I don't think it plays my kind of music."

"Oh well," said his friend and employer, "who cares about times and someone that long ago? Especially old gaffer Ernest."

"Well Ernest picked up something in the news a year or so ago about there being an exhibition specially for this chap Turner 'cause he's become super famous and it said how much his paintings fetch if ever one comes on the market."

"How much?" interjected Jason quickly for he was always one to hear about money. That much at least he had learned at school and at his father's knee. He also knew almost instinctively that since the financial crash of the first decade of the new century, works of art and some other things were going up in value, or at least in price with interest rates so low on cash investments.

"Yeagh, but things like that can go down as quick as they go up!" thought Simon when he had taken this in.

"How much?" Jason reiterated. "Did Ernest say anything about that?"

"No, of course he didn't," replied Simon.

"He doesn't care about money so long as he can make his way here to The Stag and have his pint or two on his pension.

Nice thing about this village is that there are still a few old families here despite the second homes and incomers. At least we help to keep the Stag open alongside all the walkers and campers who like its real ale choices, especially the 3 x 3rds pallet choice written over the bar there. Personally I prefer three times a full pint choice when I've finished a hard day's work in the fields, though it's a lot easier than it used to be with fewer machines. I wouldn't be without my quad bike especially when it comes to rounding up sheep off the fells."

***

Not many villages are so unspoilt and still have more than one working farm in the middle of what visitors rightly reckon to be one of the most beautiful in the north of England, thought Simon.

"That chap Auden said as much and he knew a thing or two about Dufton. Built in our wonderful red sandstone too. And that's saying something. He described High Cup Nick as 'one of the holiest places of the earth', we were told at school. Mind you I don't believe the local legend that St Cuthbert's body was brought this way from Lindisfarne to escape the invading Vikings and up past High Cup to Dufton Fell on its way east. Why should it have been even though Bede tells of it being carted around the borders? Anyway, having ended up in Durham Cathedral you could say that it rests in a place built by man to the glory of God whereas High Cup Nick is a place made by God to be gloried in by man."

Simon turned to his beer with a barely hidden grin as he felt a bit proud of this clever remark and his little speech. He may not have had much in the way of formal education, but he often amazed his friend with his memory and ability to think original thoughts, especially over a pint or two after a hard day in the fields. Jason wasn't taking much notice, however. True to form he'd been thinking there may be a chance to make some money.

"Well," said Jason after a while, "I reckon if Turner made it to one of those big exhibitions in London he must have been OK. There could be enough info for those chaps I met in Carlisle a month or two ago who were searching for bargains in the art world. I reckon I have a number on my phone from one of the guys who asked me to keep an eye open. What say we try to find out more about this couple over there and make a bit on the side offering information to those guys? But for now let's hold on till we've got enough gen to sell at a decent price."

But Simon wouldn't hear of it. He hadn't spent those hours in the Methodist Sunday School for nothing as far as his honesty was concerned, but he drew the line at their teetotal admonishments, considering that refreshment at the Stag was a necessity after a day's graft on the farm.

***

Edward sidled up to the lads and offered to buy a round. They were not averse to that, even if it was offered by a 'foreigner'.

"Would you mind if I interrupted? Does anyone around here know something of the history of these parts?" said this rather urbane gent from other parts, possibly even from the South. Not even his walking gear and boots could completely hide that.

"Do people ever speak of a visit to Dufton by the artist

Turner many years ago?"

"Ay, course they do," opined Simon, dropping into a more vernacular style of speech for the benefit of a southerner!

"It's only 200 years ago and things change pretty slow up 'ere." There's this old boy at t'other end of the village who says his granfather telt him that *his* granfather met Turner in this very room. You should talk to old Ernest in the village. Word is he's ninety-two. He's from generations of farmers here and knows a lot even if he talks in a bit of a local way."

"What!" said Edward and Rhoda together, "Are you saying there is third-hand memory that the painter was here in this inn?"

"Do you think this man might be willing to talk to us about that," went on an excited Edward who for the first time began to dare to think that the trail may be warming.

"Oh ay he sometimes talks about nothing else when he's 'ad 'is pint or two."

"What's he called and where does he live?"

"You don't need to bother over that. He'll be 'ere for 'is pint afore you go."

Edward and Rhoda were now really excited that for the first time in their trip they may be getting close to some knowledge which might offer a clue to their search. Could it be that they were just about to make a direct link with Turner in his travels of 200 years ago? Did he really sit in this very room, perhaps on his way down from High Cup Nick? Would there be any clue as to his movements thereafter? Edward knew that Appleby was on Turner's list to visit, for he was commissioned to do so by the terms of his contract with his publisher.

"But what did he do there?" thought Edward as he drained

his glass.

"Rhoda, dear, I'm sure I'm going to need the support of another glass of this brew before confronting the old man. Do you think you might be willing to do the driving back to Appleby?"

"Oh yes," thought Rhoda, "I wondered when the short straw might be mentioned." How many times had she made the small sacrifice of refusing a second glass or had none at all! On this occasion she did feel that it might be vital for Edward to stay relaxed and calm before embarking on a venture of this potential significance.

***

At last the old man arrived and shuffled with the aid of his stick to his reserved shepherd's chair in the corner. Edward confronted him with a pint of Jennings in each hand. With a broken body from decades of grafting but still with a bright eye and a will, nay a wish to talk, this venerable figure could manage to sip and enjoy his well-earned refreshment.

Edward and Rhoda are reminded, as they look at their interlocuter, of recent proposals by the present government to raise pensionable age to seventy and gradually beyond. With her much publicised love of fell walking, perhaps the previous prime minister at least would realise the folly of imposing the same rules on physically stressed manual workers as on those around her with careers achieved in the comfort of offices in the city or in the Westminster 'bubble'.

Turns out that when Ernest was a lad his grandfather told him that *his* grandfather before him had as a boy of ten helped the ostler at the Buck Inn as it then was named. Also his future grandmother as a young girl helped with cleaning and other jobs there. Great-great-grandfather had overheard Turner telling the landlord that he was going on to Appleby and needed his horse Hector (what a name for a horse - the groom had no notion of the origin of the name). Moreover, he intended, after fulfilling his duties by sketching, to visit the castle. Bit by bit, Edward learnt of how Ernest's ancestor described Turner as a rather quiet man, more concerned with his horse and the next stages of his journey than with chatting in the yard of the inn. He did discover, however, from the young lass that she had seen the artist carefully drying out sketches from his bag, whilst muttering about High Cup Nick. There clearly wasn't any way in which this man sitting before Edward and Rhoda would have invented this wonderful story.

Could it be that they were hearing of the drawings, later to be found in the British Museum collection? Could it be that a painting had been conceived in this very place?

***

Ernest began to warm to the idea that he was the centre of attention.

"E's not only 'un as cum t' Dufton fro' other parts. I mysen talked to a fella named Auden – a bit of a poet, they sez. But 'e were no saint like t'other who were carted thro' 'ere a couple of centuries 'fore yon Auden chap. Mind thee, at least Auden were well alive but t'other poor fella were long de'ed. Name of Cuthbert they say, 'e were a saint on 'is way to his coffin in Durham. Not so many saints there now I've 'erd tell sin' all them stoodents cum." That pronouncement gave Ernest the chance to pause and suck his teeth.

"Gramps tell as 'ows Master Turner sent summat to gi' to the 'igh and mighty lord at t'castle in Appleby. But 'e says as 'ow t'lord 'ad off to France an' needed it n' more. So it got to t'ousekeeper oo arsked gret-gret-gramps oo were working at castle by then as a servant to shuv it somweers. 'E reckoned it wer' likely a paintin' but in a gradely box. 'E stuffed it in t' servants' place at back o' stables 'e sez. Anyweres 'e never reckoned them 'pressionists. Gramps sed as it were one of them writing boxes."

Edward had no qualms in offering each round if it helped the recollections of this wonderful old man. Anyway it was very good beer and much cheaper than in Berkhamsted. With origins in the North, he had understood most of what Ernest had to say, though much of it passed over Rhoda.

CHAPTER 18

While Rhoda and Edward were enjoying their supper at the Stag they were completely unaware of an insignificant car heading fast to town. The small car was parked at a pub quite near to Rhoda and Edward's hotel. If they had been there they would have recognised getting out of the car one of the young men to whom they had spoken not long before at the Stag. They would have seen him meeting a friend and becoming engaged in animated conversation over a pint or two of Jennings.

"It's a damn good job we could meet here, George before you headed back to Dufton," said Jason.

It was not at all surprising that Jason knew George, the odd job man at the castle. There had been a tradition of young men from the village working there because the Thanets had also owned Dufton Hall for two centuries. They knew that the village was an excellent source of servants, not least because they largely controlled the village affairs until the mining companies arrived. That was why the servants involved at the Stag (Buck) and castle in Turner's time knew one another well and exchanged gossip.

"I'm jolly glad we go back to being lads together," said Jason. "I think I can trust you after these many years with a big story?"

Georges' eyes lit up. Despite his work in such splendid surroundings, big stories didn't often come his way. Still in his late teens he rather idolised the older man and felt a bit more grown up that he was being trusted.

"I'm wanting some help from you George, but it must be in the strictest secrecy."

"Tell me more. Is it going to be a bit of an adventure?"

"Well it might be, if we can pull it off," whispered Jason conspiratorially. "I can't tell you how, but I've heard of a treasure that might be hidden up at the castle and I want to know if you will help me find it." He didn't think any more information was needed to get George on board.

From eager, rather boy like excitement George was now beginning to look rather doubtful, even fearful.

"Treasure," he said. "There are lots of treasures at the castle and I'm trusted there with them. I don't think I should hear any more."

Jason had anticipated some reluctance and he had been working out on the way down how he might counter it.

"Don't worry George. This doesn't really have anything to do with the castle now," he said disingenuously. "It is about an old box that got left there a couple of centuries ago and nobody at the castle even knows it might be there." Jason hadn't heard Ernest describe it as a writing box.

For all his innocence, George was no fool.

"If nobody knows about it, how do you, and does anybody else?"

Jason had to admit that Simon might have a clue but dismissed it on the grounds that he probably hadn't thought any more about it. In any case he wouldn't snitch before the job was done, for it had to be dealt with fast that very evening. Before that couple from South get their act together tomorrow, he thought.

"Well, I'll listen Jason, and I won't break the secret but I need to know what you want me to do and whether it is right to do it."

"Good man," said Jason. "I wouldn't ask you to break faith with your employer up there. She will never know."

He knew fine well that though she might not, what he was proposing was to steal an object from her property.

"Somewhere in the stables might be an old box thrown out 200 years ago. I did say treasure, but it's not like jewels or anything, just some old paper that might have rotted by now," offered Jason. Having got George's attention he was now playing down any importance of the matter. And was giving no clue as to the box's possible real content.

"Would you be prepared to see if you can find an old box looking undisturbed for so long? You haven't got much time 'cause I think someone else may be on to it. I expect it will be about the size of a vegetable box at the supermarket and just about as interesting.

"If it really is nothing more than an old box with a few bits of paper in it," said George, "I will have a look right now and if I find anything I'll bring it down here before closing time tonight."

With that they parted.

***

George did find a box in the stables that night, indeed one section had several such boxes. They seemed to be like the old family travelling boxes of the Thanet family which he had seen stacked in the stables some time ago. Most of them were quite big but one of them was about the right size. It wasn't very heavy and was securely locked. The others were much bigger than Jason had described. A quick search of other rooms in the stables revealed mainly old furniture and some gardening tools and a few ancient-looking bicycles. He was able to easily sneak out the smaller box and head down to the pub with it. Jason was waiting anxiously until George arrived and made sure that Jason had the box that night in exchange for £20.

It wasn't long before Jason was on the phone to his acquaintance in Carlisle.

"Is that Christopher? Is it safe for me to talk over the phone? I reckon I've got something to interest you; an old painting. Can you meet me in Penrith first thing tomorrow and bring some tools to get us into a locked box? We can meet on the garage forecourt on the left as you come into town from the A66."

As he drove to meet his contact Jason considered how he might gain as much as possible from his proposed rather shady dealings with the arts world. He was well aware that his conjectures were totally a consequence of overhearing private conversations at the Stag. But with the finding of the box by George, he was beginning to feel more and more confident that he was on the track of a windfall.

Next morning two cars converged on Penrith, each driver with hope of a deal.

PART 5

He who would search for pearls must dive below
John Dryden

CHAPTER 19

Despite their exciting day in the hills, Edward would not be kept awake back at their hotel especially after their hike and a few local ales. Rhoda spent much of the night tossing and turning while she digested the information gleaned at The Stag. Could it really be that somewhere in the castle might be a box with a precious painting? Even if there was, could it have survived these 200 years of careless storage? She was already beginning to be thrilled with the excitement of the chase. Edward was outwardly calmer but determined after breakfast to go back to the castle. First he ordered two boiled eggs on the principle that the best test of any hotel was whether they could serve eggs 'à point'. They could, and he started the day with optimism. Certainly a return visit to the castle was essential.

"I thought we should keep the information we got from old Ernest strictly to ourselves for the time being," said Edward, "at least the part about the box being delivered to the castle. Clearly he has told the story to many people of Turner's visit to Dufton. But hopefully we are the only ones who know about the box. Nevertheless I can't see any option other than being completely straight with the owner of the castle and telling her about old Ernest's memories even if they might be completely false," admitted Edward to Rhoda over toast and marmalade.

"Of course," she readily agreed. "I think we should ask

the manager here if he can put us in touch with the castle management."

Two days ago they had been shown round as tourists and had been told that the last Thanet to own and live in the building had sold the property in 1962.

***

When it was explained that his guests wished to meet the castle resident privately and an outline, but no details given of their mission, the manager responded promptly.

"I do know," he said immediately, "that she is in residence because she is very much involved in town affairs as I am. So I am able to speak to her easily and will get a message to her forthwith. Complete your breakfast whilst I do so. I can heartily recommend our Cumbrian sausage if your appetites will run to that so early in the day. Perhaps you would share one with a taste of tomato and mushroom."

They acquiesced and soon it arrived with half its coil on Edward's plate and the other half on Rhoda's, disconnected, of course!

"Well that's an excellent start," enthused Rhoda. "If the rest of the day goes half as well we may be in luck."

"I do hope you are right," breathed the much more cautious partner in the adventure.

"The more I reflect, the more unlikely it seems to be that Ernest is completely right about his memories and even more so that the recollections of his grandfather and *his* before him are to be trusted. The chain of connection is so long. Even if Chinese whispers are not involved, anything could have happened along the track of 200 years of castle history."

Soon they were assured that the lady of the castle would meet them at the gate in half an hour's time.

***

As they made their way again up Boroughgate to the imposing entry archway to the castle grounds Edward had to admit to being somewhat intimidated by the grandeur of his surroundings, but he need not have feared. They were warmly welcomed by the lady of the castle who introduced herself as Caroline and insisted on them being informal. They didn't feel at all comfortable with that suggestion but she absolutely insisted. Before long they were enjoying morning coffee in the private apartment wing.

"So, how may I help you? I'm rather intrigued to hear more if your visit has something to do with the history of my home," they were asked after more detailed confidential explanations had been given of the general reason why they were there.

Rhoda left the talking to Edward because she felt that it was very much his project that was at stake.

Edward embarked on his story.

"It's hard to believe that we had the great good luck to meet a very old man in Dufton who claimed that his ancestor, let's call him James, had met J. M. W. Turner in the Stag Inn, then known as The Buck. James said he had heard Turner arranging with the groom to have his horse ready to ride into town.

"A couple of years later James graduated to working at the castle. The servants had this story of how an important man delivered something in a wooden writing box to the lord of the castle but it was left in the hands of the housekeeper pending the return of the lord who was away in France. The story was that it had something to do with the painter. We have reason to believe that it could have contained a painting being delivered to Lord Thanet. Much later, a servant was asked to stack the box in the stable block because the lord never did return."

"When was this?" demanded Caroline.

"Well, I think it would have been some short time after the summer of 1818 when records show Turner being back visiting his friend and patron Wilfred Fawkes at Farnley Hall near Otley. He used to visit practically every year."

Rhoda was quietly impressed by the extent of Edward's research in the archives of the British Library. Most of this detail of Turner's travels was new to her. Edward liked to keep some of his hobby knowledge quietly to himself until it came of use.

"The castle archives in the muniments room are in rather good condition and I had them organised a year or two ago by a local young woman who was working on a dissertation covering most of the nineteenth century activities in the castle. She did an excellent job and it would be easy for me to check any addition to our inventory about then. Could you return in an hour or two? In the meantime you may like to wander round the grounds and see Lady Anne Clifford's bee-house down towards the river. It's a sort of square building with a pyramid-shaped roof."

That gave Edward and Rhoda opportunity to carefully discuss whether they could be totally confident of Caroline's integrity over matters of this kind. They quickly came to the conclusion that they could be.

***

The trio re-assembled at the appointed time and it was already obvious that Caroline was becoming a little animated and anxious to continue her involvement.

"Wait for it," she dramatically announced. "A handsome mahogany writing slope was added to the castle inventory in the summer of 1818! I can't tell you any more for there is no record of it since then."

Edward and Rhoda's spirits had risen only to be dashed.

"Could it be," questioned Edward, "that it be thrown into low-grade storage?" He had the stable block in mind.

"Yes, it certainly could," rejoined Caroline. "You see in a house as big as this, quite small objects like that would often cease to be used when their utility expired with fashion, and might easily be retired. They were not considered 'antique' and collectable at the time. I'm definitely up for the hunt if you care to explore the far reaches of the property," she smiled. "Let me change into something a bit more practical and I'll gladly join you and the spiders in the stable block.

***

Left alone for a few minutes, Edward and Rhoda couldn't hide their excitement as the temperature of the chase rose. Normally rather staid, particularly in such splendid surroundings, they felt driven to dance a minuet such as they felt would have graced this building in the early nineteenth century.

"What on earth are we doing?" choked Edward between laughs. "We haven't found anything yet and even if we do, why should an old writing slope be of any significance?" Rhoda was more sanguine but hopping from foot to foot with excitement.

"Edward," she pronounced. "Isn't it a fantastic coincidence that I should have bought a Gillow writing slope only six months ago? But not so much of a coincidence, perhaps," she cunningly continued. "Don't you remember me telling you that I had found a pencilled signature on the bottom of the drawer in mine? It was quite easily deciphered and was that of a journeyman called W. Naylor who worked for Gillows at that time. I was able to check it in the archives in Lancaster. It listed Naylor as having made *two* writing slopes of the same size as mine in 1792.

"Now," she declared with the lowest sign of sensationalism she could muster in the circumstances but drawing the maximum drama by her body language, "one of those was delivered to a Mr Fawkes of Farnley Hall in Yorkshire as a follow-up to a package of furniture he ordered in 1792 from the Lancaster workshop!"

How she loved to share in the sheer thrill which she saw on Edward's usually unexpressive face. Edward was trying to quell his flights of fancy and struggling to bring his emotions under control.

"Rhoda," he said as sternly as he could and as much to himself as her, "we are grown up. We mustn't allow ourselves to behave like children. After all Caroline will be back in a moment and we still haven't found this object and even if we had, there need be no link to Turner. Let's at least be prepared for a huge let-down."

As usual Edward's glass was half empty, or as he would have it, there was need for calm. They agreed, though that their host could not have been more helpful.

CHAPTER 20

Caroline's idea of practicality was jodhpurs and a pink shirt. She was definitely ready for the hunt.

"I had thought of exploring the attics but the previous owners did a fair job of sorting them out."

At that Edward's heart sank again. Although the stables had been mentioned by Ernest, he couldn't really countenance such a precious item condemned to that fate.

"The stables must be our first objective in view of your friend's memories. Anyway I rarely need to go there unless the groom has a problem with one of the horses."

She led the way across the large courtyard to the stable block. Their previous tour had not included these. It reminded Edward of the stabling of horses or carriages as he had seen at Tatton and was a similar large building as was required in those days. It was arranged around an inner second courtyard.

"That side is where the horses lived and my two still do," explained Caroline, "and this side was for the coaches. One remains for the public to see but the other doors hide my more modern transport. It's more convenient cranking up a Range Rover than hooking two or four horses to a carriage even if my groom could do it in less than an hour or so," she clucked, enough to disturb the few hens taking refuge there from the wind.

"Let us follow your lead and tackle the servants' quarters on the other two sides. Most of these tiny rooms are either full of junk or full of much worse. We don't really have need for them any more. Fortunately Edward and Rhoda had been advised in the invitation from Caroline to come in suitable dress to enjoy an informal visit. She was not herself a very formal person as their advisor back at the hotel knew from his links in local affairs.

The three of them worked their way down the two remaining sections of the building. Edward and Rhoda could hardly believe how much domestic debris accumulated in such a place until they ruefully remembered how much there was in their own small loft at home.

All around them were the signs of energetic activity of small animals of all kinds which these chambers supported. Rhoda didn't mind the spiders and their webs too much or the layers of dust, but she did draw the line at scurrying small rodents, mainly wood mice which were fairly omnivorous. She couldn't rid herself of the thought that if they did find the object of their search it could not have escaped all their attentions.

Caroline was the first to spot some disturbance in one of the rooms.

"Come and look here," she called to Rhoda, "these old travelling boxes seem to have been very recently disturbed. I can't think why. I haven't given any orders to clear these rooms."

Both of them admitted to a sinking feeling. Had someone got there before them? There was no doubt that dust and cobwebs had recently been disturbed amongst a pile of the boxes. They could see a distinct oblong shape about two feet long and a little over one foot wide clear of dust on the top of an extremely dirty, much larger box amongst others of similar size. There were streaks in the remaining dust showing that whatever had occupied the newly revealed clean patch had been dragged away and had gone.

When Edward had been called and the situation discussed, it is hardly surprising that doubts began to set in. The three had to agree that it looked very disappointing, even suspicious.

Edward was the first to put into words their collective fears.

"Is there any way in which someone could have got wind of our search and its objective?" he said. Privately he was searching his memory for any person or persons who may have overheard any relevant conversations. First and foremost was the question of whether Caroline could be trusted completely. They had already considered this question and nothing had happened to change his mind. A lifetime of work as a solicitor had made Edward a very good judge of character and he remained sure of her. He felt that there was a greater likelihood of someone having overheard their conversation with old Ernest at the Stag. Again he had decided with Rhoda that his word was to be trusted, and though he had not specifically been sworn to secrecy, he was a man of few words which did not pour out without encouragement. That left the couple from Leeds and the two young fellows at the bar. He had no reason to suppose that the two caravanners would take much notice of a conversation in the far end of the room slightly divided by the entrance porch from the bar end. But perhaps the two young men had very sharp ears and may have listened in?

"Could two young fellows in the bar at the Stag have gained access to the castle last night?" he quizzed Caroline. She was adamant that they could not.

On those grounds Edward proposed that at the very least they should continue the search. All three agreed, but with markedly less enthusiasm than half an hour before.

Soon Edward found himself in a room with abandoned large presses of a similar period to the sought-after box. He opened each one on the creaking broken hinges to reveal the linen slides.

One after another they yielded nothing of interest. Then at the back of one of the slides he could see the face of an object of very dark coloured wood about two feet long and eight inches high. It was heavy, but feeling around its sides he realised that it had a strong brass handle at each end.

"Rhoda," he shouted, "could this old piece of junk be the twin of your wonderful campaign desk?"

The shout was enough to shake Rhoda right out of her minutes of doubt perched on a wicker chair straight out of *A Passage to India*. Could her fears be misplaced?

"Coming," she sang. "Where are you?"

"I'm here," came a muffled voice from the back of nowhere in the next cubicle.

Together they dragged out the find into daylight and Caroline flourished a duster from somewhere.

"Oh, Edward," whispered Rhoda. "Look at that Spanish mahogany. Even in this state it is beginning to glow with the light on it. If it isn't a twin to mine it is jolly close. The handles are the same swan-neck, the brass skeleton escutcheon is the same, the drawer at this end, the left as we face the lock, looks the same depth and width."

Rhoda was rapidly getting carried away. So many times

had she rehearsed this moment showing off her specimen to admiring friends. She felt she had pretty well mastered the jargon.

"Caroline," said Edward, trying to mask the urgency in his voice. "This is yours. Is it possible for us to look inside?"

"It most certainly would be," she replied, "if we had a key. It is clearly locked. "Ah," she cried, "at least we can pull open the drawer. It doesn't have a lock," as she vainly tugged at the left hand swan-neck.

"No you can't," said Rhoda. "if it's like mine, as I'm convinced it is, the drawer has a secret release which cannot be activated until the box is open."

All three were now brimming with anticipation, indeed all four since Caroline's odd job man had joined them.

"Look," said Edward, "we don't want to do any harm. You must agree that this slope just doesn't look much damaged from its experience. Being at the back of that shelf has probably protected it from the worst. Maybe yours has been abandoned a time or two in its history, Rhoda, but you wouldn't know now that it has been lovingly cleaned and waxed. Is there any chance of getting an expert to open this up for us, Caroline? A little patience at this stage should be the order of the day."

"George!" called Caroline to her man. "Will you drop down into town and get Walter the locksmith to come up? After all he's no stranger to rush jobs at the castle, generally on old locks."

Edward thought that it really did look in decent condition after all.

"What sort of state will these buildings have been kept in whilst in use and since?" he said.

Caroline had, of course, taken expert advice about the condition of all aspects of the property when considering the biggest, and undoubtedly most exciting and demanding thing in her life.

"The stables have always seemed very dry and dusty since we moved here in the early years of the new millennium. The roof is in very good trim and the boiler house has been here for decades. The Thanets had a good reputation for looking after things. Let's take it over to the house. Goodness, it's very heavy, isn't it?"

"Gillows didn't do things by halves," smiled Rhoda. "These small furnishings were made out of the finest woods obtainable at the time and were strong enough, not only to fulfil their purpose as travelling desks, but as you can see to survive to the present day. Not that many have survived for so long. Most would have been destroyed in the campaigns of the 1800s such as Crimea, or lost on the high seas. Most of the rest just fell out of fashion."

CHAPTER 21

Another cup of tea was called for to speed the inevitable wait. It gave Rhoda her chance to give a little account to Caroline of what seemed to be the matching slope at home in Hertfordshire. Quickly she outlined why she thought that two matching ones had been made by the same craftsman at the same time. Careful measurements would help to support that because the Gillow archives listed quite a number of similar objects but the exact dimensions varied with the order and requirements of the customer. There were sometimes extra fittings in the desks, especially when they were to be used as campaign desks doubling up as gentlemen's toiletry stores. She could have enthused for much longer were she not now feeling something of a reaction to such an exciting morning and to the stress of waiting to see inside.

"Ladies," Edward said, "we may be hoping to see a Turner soon but Rhoda and I have just been studying your Euonymus Bush in the garden, Caroline, which brought to mind Hieronymus Bosch!" To his secret joy Caroline between guffaws said, "Please bee-hive, Edward". The ice was broken.

A glance at Edward made Rhoda feel that his usually calm demeanour might be rocked also. Quickly she was relieved to hear him relapse with a deadpan face into his infuriating habit of punning. She had always suspected that her original attraction to him had been the thought of combining Rhoda with Dendron!

***

Two brews of tea later, George arrived with Walter the locksmith.

"Afternoon Miss Caroline. What is it this time?" he grinned. Clearly he was quite used to being summoned to the castle. It was his favourite source of really interesting work. Old locks could be a challenge, and that made his day.

"Can you get into this one, Walter without damage? We don't know what it might contain."

"Show me the lock I can't overcome," he confidently said.

These country craftsmen had vast experience and wide interest in their very varied work. Caroline made a thing of cultivating such skills.

That little case of his revealed a fascinating collection of old keys from at least a couple of centuries and mysterious hooks and keeper wedges. In a seemingly impossibly brief time the tense observers heard a sharp click and Walter carefully lifted the lid a few millimetres.

"Now Miss Caroline. Who is to have the satisfaction of lifting it right open?"

Although it technically belonged to Caroline she gamely offered the opportunity to the man who had brought the project to this point with his quiet insistence on following all trails.

"Carry on Edward," was her calm response.

It could hardly sound less poignant than Nelson's similar plea to Admiral Collingwood, the man who some consider won the Battle of Trafalgar.

"Thank you very much, Walter. Send me your bill, please." With this he was gently dismissed in case he got wind of the hoped-for contents.

By now young George was beginning to feel ashamed. Could this box be the one Jason was after? If so, he had got things very much wrong in giving him the other one, but could feel relieved that perhaps the real treasure had now been found and that no real harm was done. Also he had sent Jason on a wild goose chase in return for £20. He had two courses of action. One was to return the money to Jason, and the other to confess to Miss Caroline. He postponed both for a while until his courage returned. For now he crept away quietly, but strained to overhear and see as much as he could as the contents were explored.

***

It is hard to understand how an individual in retirement from a stressful job carried out without alarm for so many years could find the simple task of opening an old box to require so much courage. How could the onlookers feel so much strain when they were all hoping for a joyous moment? It was the anticipation of failure, of acute disappointment which held them all in thrall. Did it really matter so much? Aren't we aware that the prize may never have existed? Of course, but doesn't hope still spring eternal? Edward felt as if he may be giving that new life to a creation held in suspense for 200 years.

Ever so carefully Edward eased open the lid and temporarily propped it up with the adjustable brass fitting enabling it to be variously angled so that the top of the box, with its detachable ledge could support reading matter conveniently. It was an exact replica of Rhoda's possession even down to the two glass ink bottles in the front compartments although one of them was broken. It also still showed its original baize writing surface so at least that hadn't been disturbed in 200 years. There was no sign of mould. With the lid completely open, Rhoda suggested that they inspect any contents of the drawer. Caroline gently tugged at its swan-neck handle with no effect.

"It really is jammed," she muttered again with disappointment.

Edward motioned to Rhoda to reveal her trick. Grasping a small brass knob protruding from the top edge of the box which had not been at all accessible or visible with the lid locked, she triumphantly withdrew it and motioned to Caroline to pull the drawer open. There were a few scraps of wrinkled, slightly yellowed paper in it but they looked no more than old letters of no consequence except that one was signed Walter Fawkes. Proof, if any was needed, that they probably had the right ('write' – thought Edward silently) slope. But no sign of a painting or even a sketch. More disappointment, getting more acute each time.

"Is there any other part where a sheet of paper might be stored, Rhoda?" came from a now anxious Edward.

"Yes there is."

They watched in trepidation as she carefully pulled at a very small leather tab at the top end of the baize. It lifted on the hinge of the felt and as it came away they knew that they were seeing larger and more carefully stowed papers about the size of a small, unframed piece of art. Edward knew that Turner at that time liked to aim at about eight by twelve inches for the finished work if it was not for engraving. Most of the products of his 1817 Rhine journey were about that size, much smaller than the finished works from his 1816 trip required for engraving in the Richmondshire series.

All this went through his mind like a flash as he composed himself to ever so gently lift out the papers and place them reverently on Caroline's Pembroke table. There were three sheets. The top one proved to be blank on both sides and was clearly for protection. The second was blank on the upper exposed surface. Gently turning it over drew amazed gasps from all three of the onlookers, for before them in unfaded glory was a watercolour with the characteristic scraping-out of a Turner of the second decade of the nineteenth century! Were they looking at a clever fake set up for them to 'discover'?

Edward reviewed all the evidence to the contrary. Both he and Rhoda had accepted old Ernest's story just as they had accepted his complete integrity. From then on, each step in the chase had logically carried them forward to the next without any of the players being able to anticipate the outcome. Edward would have liked to have been a barrister if he were more eloquent, but he did quietly think of himself as having forensic skills and undoubtedly he had been highly regarded by colleagues in his profession, modestly executed in sleepy Berkhamsted.

"Could the young fellows in the bar at the Stag have overheard anything?" Even if they had, he assured himself they could have had no part in ensuring that a 1792 Gillow writing desk would have found its way to Caroline's stables. In any case it had clearly not been opened for a century or two.

***

Caroline was bustling to transfer an anglepoise lamp from on top of a bureau across the room and setting it up over the table.

For a short exposure its rather dim light would not damage this delicate work.

Just visible were the initials JMWT at the top right-hand corner.

Edward brought to mind his homework in the British Museum and the Turners seen at the Tate. He had admired and studied them for decades and would not be confused with a replica so easily. A replica of what? Spread before them was a striking image of High Cup in extremely stormy weather, impossible to create by anyone before or after Turner. Here was a relatively early work of the artist showing those skills in depth which he so effectively used later in his life in watercolours and oils. And completely unknown to the art world.

Edward felt that it just had to be right. It must be the object of his quest. The most important point to him was the correspondence of the two sketches in the BM and this scene before them. It must have been a product of that journey in 1816 since he was known not to have returned to those wild parts. Caroline and Rhoda imbibed the atmosphere in the room from just a few glances at Edward as he sat immobile nearby. The time had passed for juvenile glee.

If he was right, this had to be the find of the century, most of the previous whole century in fact, since scholars had become confident of fully recording the known works of the master. Of course it would have to be authenticated by the world's Turner experts. Quite rightly no one would take notice of an amateur attribution, but the chain of events leading to its discovery gave Edward some quiet satisfaction.

As Edward sat transfixed, and Rhoda basked in the vicarious pleasure which she felt, Caroline had briefly disappeared. Within minutes she was busying herself taking flutes from a wall cupboard and, after an appropriate pop, filling them with bubbly. It wasn't deemed an occasion for the Prosecco when brut was in stock.

Grasping the significance of the moment and taking on board Edward and Rhoda's joint enthusiasms, she raised her glass to:

"Mr Turner and Mr Gillow."

Edward joined in outwardly cool but in reality more alive than he had felt since retirement. Rhoda was secretly delighted to have Richard Gillow bracketed with Turner for this purpose. She knew that this second master of the family firm had died five years before this painting could have been made, but nineteen years after supervising the making of the desk before them, over the shoulder of his son Robert. Here were two special examples of different art forms originating in the northern counties and by two men undoubtedly known to each other through their common patron, Walter Fawkes. He must be the link, they all thought, behind the remarkable coincidences bringing together Rhoda's and Edward's different hobbies and enthusiasms.

CHAPTER 22

Edward admitted that he hadn't got as far as considering what may happen if the unimaginable occurred and the supposed missing Turner was found. Three people knew about it. For the immediate future he was very concerned that it should be in safe hands until authenticated. There could be no question of any other action for the time being.

"Caroline," he began, "this was found on your property. May I propose that it stays here in your safekeeping whilst we consider what to do next? After all, a castle should be a pretty safe place to hold a treasure for a few more days when it has survived being here for a couple of centuries."

At this moment he didn't know what her reaction to the find might be when the complexity of it had sunk in. Indeed he didn't understand the situation himself despite his legal background. A number of possibilities suggested themselves, but he kept them to himself at this juncture.

Could it be the property of those who had found it following the evidence?

Was it owned by the present owner of the building in which it was found?

Did the descendants of the man who had left it here so long ago have a right to it?

Where did the Thanet family, a member of which had commissioned but never paid for it, come in?

Was it really the property of the surviving members of the

Turner family since J. M. W. had never received any fee for this work?

How did the rules about Treasure Trove apply to a situation like this?

His musings were interrupted by Caroline.

"I think we have all three had a very exciting day," she concluded. "I shall be very happy to look after the painting. After all we are all witnesses of the find and as long as you can trust me not to cause any damage to it, I hope you will both be happy with that. For now, I shall see you out of the main gate. You don't have far to go to your beds. May I wish you both a calm and happy night's rest. The castle isn't open at all tomorrow so we can re-convene at a time which suits, without interruption. May I invite you for morning coffee? I will be at the gate at ten thirty."

***

Edward and Rhoda made their way down Boroughgate hardly needing to speak. They both knew pretty well what the other was thinking. Back in the quiet of their room they confirmed their mutual feelings of trust of Caroline and confidence that something good would be bound to emerge. After all, the big challenge, namely to see if Edward's supposition might have any truth, had been spectacularly met. Anything else would be icing on the cake. Whose cake it was could be resolved, they were sure. With that assurance they both slept well, looking forward to porridge in the morning. It was strange how the farther north people travelled in the British Isles, the more they demanded porridge for breakfast. Rhoda wondered if the Scots lose their taste for it if they were travelling south? She certainly felt confident that the porridge served here hardly thirty miles from the border would be of the highest quality.

"Edward dear," she said, over the breakfast table, "I'd recommend starting what may be a stressful day with porridge."

A slightly startled Edward thought for a moment and then happily placed his order. Neither of them were in the least bit disappointed. Thus armed, they retraced their steps up Boroughgate to find Caroline waiting at the castle gate. With their only real experience of castles being the ruin of twelfth-century Berkhamsted Castle near home it seemed so many centuries away from this morning's welcome at the gate of a real, lived-in castle. It served to remind them vividly of why they were there, following Edward's hero of a mere two centuries before.

***

"Good morning Caroline," came from both. They felt at home now with their host, but still not very comfortable joining her in such grand surroundings.

"Do come through to my private apartments," she invited. "Let's enjoy our coffee and biscuits together to prepare us for what I hope will be a constructive discussion of where we go from here."

Despite their misgivings, Edward and Rhoda soon relaxed and thoroughly enjoyed their brief encounter with someone living in such a fine building. It was such a different experience for them compared with touring the castle as members of a small guided public tour.

"That was only three days ago," thought Edward. "We had no anticipation that we would now need to be thinking of what should be done in this strangest of circumstances. Reality is so often completely different from dreaming."

Nothing could have prepared them for this moment. His thoughts were suddenly interrupted by Caroline saying:

"I have one first suggestion to make. The nearest Turner expertise of which I am aware is at the Abbot Hall Gallery in Kendal. I think we should take the painting to ask their opinion. There seems little point of any further concern if it turns out to be insignificant, I mean not even a Turner at all."

Curiously Rhoda was the first to react to this sensible idea. That was not because of Turner, but because she recognised that gallery as being the home of a fine collection of Gillow furniture. Funny how deep-seated interests almost eclipse the most exciting new ones when such coincidences arise. Edward's thoughts were going off in a different direction. He remembered clearly that a very well-known Turner watercolour was in the collection there, namely the 1804 *The Passage of Mount St. Gothard.*

Neither of them needed any further encouragement from Caroline.

"As it happens," she was saying, "I do have some acquaintance with an expert there through our mutual interest in promoting cultural tourism in Cumbria and would be happy to phone him immediately to make an appointment if that is what you would like. Kendal is little over twenty miles away and a real bonus is that we could stop off in Orton on the way back where there is a fine chocolate factory." Edward had been brought up with knowledge of Willie Wonka's enterprise and ever since had a yearning for good English chocolates; not European, which he found rather too milky and lacking in character were it not for fancy decoration. The darker the chocolate the better, he reckoned.

***

Almost before they had finished coffee, Caroline had secured a meeting at the gallery. In view of Rhoda and Edward's explanation for their joint enthusiasm, she went on to say that they should take the writing slope with them and reveal the origin and discovery of the painting after, but not before getting an independent expert view of its importance. That way they would immediately be linking the Turner and Gillow interest shared by the Dendrons and indeed by the gallery. But such synchronies are the lifeblood of the storyteller mused Caroline, and sometimes even found or at least imagined by the historian. But this wasn't a story to the three; it was the very making of history albeit in a small way.

***

Caroline shared the journey to Kendal in the Dendrons' car. A very open and scenic drive started almost as they left the castle grounds and soon they were carefully avoiding sheep lying on the warm tarmac of the unfenced road, a new experience for the travellers from Hertfordshire, apart from Edward's boyhood memories. Tebay to Kendal took them past the site of the 2007 London to Glasgow-bound express train crash at Grayrigg where Caroline described how the local villagers had cared for all the passengers until emergency services arrived. Edward couldn't help considering how much cross-country travel had changed from Turner's visit to Dufton and Appleby to the present day.

150

Leaving the driving to Edward, Rhoda was free to admire John Carr's Georgian Abbot Hall as they arrived and parked close to the extraordinarily wide parish church. She didn't know that Carr had also been active in extending Farnley Hall so the potential new Turner could have been a subject of discussion 200 years apart in two of this architect's buildings.

After introductions, the Turner scholar was ready to conduct them to his study where he questioned Caroline as to the purpose of their visit which she had not fully explained.

Edward proudly opened the folder he had brought in from the car, and laid it rather flamboyantly, it seemed to Rhoda, on the table.

"Could you please give us your view of this watercolour, Frank?" pleaded Caroline. "Afterwards I will gladly explain where it came from, if you think it is worthwhile".

As befitted a knowledgeable professional, the display before him elicited a long silence. His three visitors tried vainly to look nonchalant as they waited and didn't dare to look at one another.

"Do you know, Caroline, my first impression of this painting is…". Here followed another long and painful pause.

"I think…, I think that this is either a very fine copy, or it is an excellent example of the genius of J. M. W. Turner in his mid period, reminiscent of the style he was using in his work for Whitaker's great travel book of Richmondshire. His use of colour layers and scraping reminds me very much of his pictures in this region from that tour, many of which are housed at Farnley Hall near Otley. Especially his treatment of stormy weather. No one else could have done that. My inclination is to say that I lean towards Turner himself rather than a competent copyist of his style. Either way, the subject is unknown to me."

Noticing the visible signs of relief turning to quiet expressions of satisfaction in his visitors that he had not condemned it as of no consequence, Frank turned slowly to Caroline and begged to hear the story she had promised.

"Well, I think you should hear it from my friends Edward and Rhoda."

Caroline was pleased to sit back and watch Frank's reaction as the story unfolded. Rhoda liked to start from the very beginning of how Edward had come to set himself the objective of trying to discover if this painting did indeed exist. For his part Edward was content to let the narrative unfold. After all, Rhoda was so much better at adding a little zest to her account. Edward took over briefly when they came to recounting the interview with old Ernest and Caroline came in to describe the finding of the box. As she did so, Rhoda excused herself to nip out to the car and came back struggling a bit with the heavy writing slope. She knew that placing this before Frank would itself add to their chronicle. Indeed it did.

"That's a very fine piece," he said. "Much more than a box." This gave Rhoda her chance to expound her knowledge of such an article made by William Naylor for Gillows, together with the one in front of them.

"Of course I know about these slopes," murmured Frank, "but I expect that very few have survived their frequent use in battle or at sea. I haven't seen one before, though I believe one came up at Bonhams quite recently."

"Yes one did," declaimed Rhoda as modestly as she could; "actually I am the proud new owner of it. I treasure it greatly."

"So you should. They are a wonderful reminder both of the quality of the maker and the uses to which they were often put at that time.

"You have told a marvellous story of detective work, rare even in the world of fine art. I can only congratulate you and admire you for your tenacity."

"Oh, the latter was easy," confided Edward. "You see I have been a fan of Turner since as long as I can remember."

"Your story adds huge weight to my attribution. We couldn't ask for a better provenance. I'm sure colleagues in London will confirm what I have said."

When the significance of his remarks had sunk in, Frank spoke again:

"I believe it would be entirely appropriate for me to show you round this house with attention given to our magnificent Turner watercolours for you Edward, and our special Gillow pieces from the period of this house for you to see, Rhoda.

Caroline has often inspected our great triptych of the life of Anne Clifford, one time owner of her house. You must also see it now that your association with Appleby Castle is perhaps a little more tangible than as mere tourists, I venture to suggest, Caroline? It came from the castle where it was for more than 300 years. It looks as if your Turner may have been there for about 200 years, though hidden away."

Edward and Rhoda felt that they were being shown the possessions of a private house owner, so intimate was the display of paintings and furniture on the ground floor of the house. In addition to the *Passage of St Gothard...* Edward was delighted to see Turner's *Windermere* painted in 1821 which meant about five years after the putative *High Cup Nick* now in their hands. They were of similar size and execution so he asked Frank lots of questions to compare the two and then poured over the use of colour and scraping explained to him.

Frank remarked how bright the colours in the new find were. So few watercolours had remained completely out of daylight for 200 years.

***

Edward was busy inspecting the Romney portraits hanging in the next room and rather proudly explained the reason why. Frank was amused to hear Edward's story of having been to the same junior school as Romney, though more than 200 years apart! He congratulated Edward on his dual 'connections' with one of the foremost portrait painters, and now with undoubtedly the finest landscape artist of that time. Edward was then fascinated as Frank went on to explain that, after going to London, Romney studied at the Academy of Drawing which had been set up in the house where the young Turner later grew up!

"Do you think they ever met?" questioned Edward.

"I'm sure they would," said Frank, "their lives overlapped and Turner became an associate academician of standing like Romney long before him."

Meanwhile Rhoda was occupied in the room across the hall where she was entranced to see a superb inlaid satinwood commode and a very fine satinwood desk dating from the time of her modest writing slope and its twin from Appleby. Rhoda had hardly noticed the Romneys until Frank explained that they may well have been framed by Gillows for he was known to be a customer of theirs when he needed particularly fine frames.

"In view of the fascinating link between a Gillow piece and a Turner which you seem to have discovered," smiled

154

Frank, "I can't let you go without pointing out that the commode you so much admire is on loan from a family who lived on an Island in Windermere. So we might stretch our imagination to say there is a small second link between the Lancaster craftsmen and Turner through his painting of that lake. It was painted some five years after High Cup Nick. But we don't know if he visited the house on the island."

The three departed, more than satisfied with the support they had been given in their quest for the Turner. On Caroline's advice they were scheduled to visit the chocolate factory in Orton for refreshment on their return journey to Appleby.

CHAPTER 23

"Willie Wonka's factory had nothing on this wonderful place," enthused Edward. It was the first time he had seen his favourite confectionery being made. His normally rather inscrutable features showed his delight at finding his secret addiction so well represented.

"I'm going for the dark ones," he said predictably. Rhoda had been used for decades to finding most of the milk chocolates, and always the white chocolates, left behind in shared boxes. He was fond of claiming that 'white chocolate' was antithetic.

Sitting over mugs of chocolate in the factory cafe didn't seem to be a suitable place for the three to consider the next steps.

Caroline broke the silence.

"When we are back at the castle, I trust that you will be my guests for dinner. I think we have a few things to discuss, don't you?"

They did think so and were happy to accept.

***

"You will excuse us for an hour or so to get changed."

Edward and Rhoda hadn't been the dinner guests of the chatelaine of a real and actually rather splendid castle before. Indeed they had never in their wildest imaginations considered it likely. Rhoda was delighted with the opportunity to display her best outfit, and with the chance to needle Edward a little.

"Are you glad now that you did bring your tweed jacket," she teased. "Country styles or not, you have to admit that this is a bit special.

"Do we need to take a bottle of something for our hostess, do you think?"

"What do you think might be appropriate etiquette?" was his only reply.

Rhoda brought her common sense to bear on the conundrum.

"Caroline has been so thoughtful and kind to us that I propose that we give her the large box of chocolates I secretly bought at Orton," she rather smugly confessed.

"Has it got dark ones," Edward cheerfully followed up, "in case she hands them round?"

"Trust you. Come on, we'd better be going."

***

Caroline ushered them into the magnificent dining hall in the part of the building re-built by the Earl of Thanet in the late seventeenth century following Lady Anne Clifford leaving the property to her son-in-law. Caroline explained as they sat at the table how ironic it is that he brought much of the stone from two of her other castles to the west and east. It left both looking a little more derelict than in her time, only a decade or so before.

At first a party of three seemed overwhelmed in such a fine room until Caroline rapidly made them feel very much at home. Again she began the business which they had all expected.

"There are four of us now who know about this find and that it is highly likely to be genuine. Let's proceed on that assumption. It poses a tricky question of ownership, don't you think?" she very reasonably remarked. "Do you care for a glass of claret whilst we consider?"

Edward had already given some thought to this puzzle.

"As the person who set this ball rolling, and with Rhoda, followed it up," he modestly explained. "I feel I ought to be the first to speak."

"Of course," was readily agreed, but with some concern about how the conversation may proceed.

Edward spoke slowly and thoughtfully. He reviewed his first private thoughts on the matter when the painting was found.

"I believe we must go back to when Turner's agent is said to have left the Gillow writing desk here. Do we know who he was, I wonder? The records show that Turner was visiting his friends the Fawkes at the time near Otley. If the painting was entrusted to Fawkes then that family may have a claim, do you think? However, if Fawkes, or any other agent was asked to leave it here for Lord Thanet, could it be possible that it was commissioned by him when Turner came here in 1816?"

"If it was, and it was delivered, did Thanet pay for it?" interrupted Rhoda. "If so, does it belong to his descendants?"

"Somebody obviously didn't properly check the box and had it put out in the stables," pointed out Caroline. "That is unlikely to be the Lord Thanet of that time because he would surely know it was linked to the delivery. I suppose it could have been one of his descendants or a housekeeper. Either way it was part of the property when I came to live here, after other

158

ownership between then and the Thanets."

"That could mean," concluded Edward, "that it belongs to you."

"I appreciate you making that point but the fact is I would never have found it. I didn't even know it existed. My view is that it should be yours. After all no one else suspected that it had been painted or at least assumed that it was lost. In natural justice it should be yours."

"That is a generous comment," Edward admitted. "As a lawyer, albeit retired, I doubt if that would convince a tribunal if it came to that."

It was left to Rhoda to spell out what she and Edward had discussed together before embarking on this riddle.

"We both feel, Caroline, that our reward has been the fun of the chase. We were greatly helped by both you and old Ernest in Dufton. It would not have been found without the help of both of you. In any case we really couldn't imagine having it in our house in Berkhamsted, however nice that would be. Our joint view at the moment is that we would like to have a really good copy made of it for that purpose and the original should be placed on public display in a safe place. If it was our choice, and we hope it would be, we consider that it be hung on permanent loan in the Abbot Hall gallery in Kendal.

"We are entirely agreed on that," smiled Edward, "and if so we would additionally hope that the two sketches be hung with it, but that last does not, of course, lie with us. Obviously the legal position might have to be tested, but I'm pretty confident about that being resolved amicably if the painting does not remain in private hands. All should perhaps be subject to the agreement of the Fawkes and Thanet families. What do you think, Caroline?"

"I think that you have probably been mulling this over long before today in anticipation of a happy outcome of your search. Am I right? If so I am delighted to agree wholeheartedly with your scheme."

"In that case, Caroline, we have a further recommendation that we ask Frank whether his trustees may consider loaning it to you for agreed periods. Your visiting members of the public may then be attracted to see it along with your other treasures including the box in which it was found."

"That is a most engaging suggestion and it could go along with you coming to stay here with me from time to time, the better to enjoy it yourselves."

"Thank you so much," chorused Edward and Rhoda.

"In the meantime, of course there must be absolute checking of your friend Frank's conclusion by the best scholars on Turner in the land. We shall need to take it to London without delay for that purpose," was Edward's conclusion.

Rhoda and Edward no longer felt that it might be a case of lèse-majesté should they hope for their new friendship to blossom.

***

One man in Carlisle and another in Dufton were much less happy with their haul of a few old newspapers from a broken-open box.

CHAPTER 24

"I plan to head straight for Scotch Corner," announced Edward. "It's a good way of getting quickly across to the east, and with Turner in the boot, I don't think we should hang about. I had planned originally anyway to go that way so that we could round things off by visiting Waters Meet at Rokeby to see another Turner location."

"I agree," said Rhoda quickly. "Since we decided to take it for further authentication, I've been wanting to push on home without any messing about."

Caroline was waiting for them in the castle so that the painting in its new protective wrapper could be slipped into the car surreptitiously. Carefully stowed and with the car rug over it, they both began to feel slightly less anxious though neither would relax until Berkhamsted was reached.

"I won't delay you any more," said Caroline as she bade farewell to her two new friends, embracing Rhoda and allowing Edward to plant a discreet kiss on her cheek, but eschewing the modern tendency to present both cheeks, as if still intending to stay in the EU. All three of them wished that would happen. Edward couldn't help thinking of the freedom with which Turner did his European grand tours and the priceless products of them.

They all agreed to meet again as soon as possible. It wasn't just the women who could hardly suppress a tear.

The vast expanse of moorland on either side of the A66 over Stainmoor could not fail to impress both travellers when they had completed the climb up from Brough. In a curious way they felt rather safe with the painting as they took advantage of the dual carriageway and the feeling of wilderness surrounding them. Bypassing Bowes reminded Edward of Dickens's use of a rather austere building there as a model for Dotheboys Hall. It didn't take much effort to imagine Wackford Squeers flexing his cane and a tremulous Nicholas Nickleby trying to escape yet more abuse. The more so in the context of the twenty-first century re-visiting of more recent abuse in institutions of various kinds which so appalled Rhoda and Edward as the media exposed it.

There was agreement that a stop at Waters Meet would have to be on another occasion when the car could be safely parked without supervision.

Descent towards Scotch Corner brought much more greenery and rural tranquility and the prospect of the A1 (M) to get them home.

"I don't know about you," breathed Rhoda, "but I could do to stop at the service station at the junction."

"Me also," agreed Edward. "We'll take turns at guarding the car."

It was pretty busy on the car park but they both thought that lots of people around was the best protection against trouble with their valuable cargo. Edward eased the car into a slot backing onto the grass verge. He began to do the Quick Cryptic as Rhoda headed off across the few metres to the cafe and lavatories.

Soon she was back, given a report of no interruption, and they swapped over.

Rhoda put the radio on, settled down and waited for Edward to return, preferably with a morning coffee and a hot chocolate. She was completely unaware of someone standing just behind the car until she realised that the boot lid was open. Must be Edward returning. With it up she couldn't see anything to the rear, and in the second or two she needed to pull herself together, it was all over with nothing and no one to be seen. Suddenly came that dreadful sinking feeling. Was it Edward? She rushed round to the back of the car and saw nothing where the painting had been. She felt utterly sick.

When Edward arrived only a moment or two later, a weeping Rhoda was being comforted by a helpful couple from a nearby car. With cars entering and leaving all the time, it was clearly impossible to get the car park sealed in time to intercept anyone.

Edward alternated between administering to a distraught Rhoda and trying to make contact with the police. When he did, they seemed, although courteous and helpful, to give little hope of intercepting a completely unknown person or vehicle. Traffic police arrived quickly and interviewed the despairing Dendrons for any glimmer of fact which may help to reconstruct the scene.

For 200 years had the painting been languishing in Appleby Castle until the Dendrons' imagination had led them to search for an unknown object in an unknown location. They had felt simultaneously proud and happy to have cracked such an enigma. And now for what purpose? It had gone.

Edward dragged his shattered thoughts together as they

waited for CID from Ripon to arrive to take over. His forensic mind suggested to him that it seemed highly unlikely that this could be an opportunistic theft. How could anyone nearby have known the painting was in the car? It was not left unattended and the boot had never been opened since leaving Appleby. He passed these thoughts on to Inspector Franklin when he and his sergeant arrived. It was no good. Beyond describing events as Rhoda could recall them, there seemed no evidence of who had burgled the car and no sign of their escape. Rhoda was quietly adamant that she had never left the car, nor opened the boot from inside.

A nearby car owner said that she had seen an innocent-looking young man with a Co-op bag near the area a few minutes before she had watched the police arrive. But she couldn't be at all sure of his movements nor did she see him get into a car.

Whilst the crime scene was thoroughly checked by SOCOs, Rhoda and Edward were looked after in a private room at the service station building. How could their elation of the last day or two be so cruelly dashed now that the enormity of what had happened dawned on them? It felt like they imagined an owner of a masterpiece might feel if it was demoted by experts from being considered the work of a renowned genius to whom it had been attributed. But at least such a person would still have the picture unchanged with the same qualities so admired. All that would have been lost is the artificial monetary value placed upon it by collectors; nothing really to do with what is on the canvass. But Edward and Rhoda's loss was so much more than fiduciary.

For a long time Edward sat silent in thought but it was Rhoda who remarked that at least they were both unharmed, at least physically.

Eventually they felt able to talk rationally about their dreadful loss. The great temptation for both was to engage in the blame game although it was not normally in their natures to do so.

"Could it have gone while you were waiting in the car?" muttered Rhoda, who felt so bad that the loss was discovered when she was nominally in charge.

"Didn't you see anyone approaching? Why did you allow yourself to be distracted?" accused Edward. Slowly he remembered that in fact he had been concentrating on the cryptic clues rather than looking round. In point of fact neither had anticipated a crime. How could anyone have known what their cargo was? Was it a random theft by an opportunistic thief lying in wait for a car to be accessible to snatch – anything – and run? Was it fortuitous, or planned that the thief had chosen a moment when there was only one person in the car in the event of being confronted? Was the thief looking for a car on the edge of the park, not overlooked at the back? Would it have been safer to park in the centre surrounded by other cars?

They were advised not to speak to anyone about what had happened until given freedom to do so. The Ripon police were busy contacting the Cumbria force headquarters after the Dendrons had described the circumstances which led to the painting being in their car. Edward just hoped that the issue did not simply fall between the two county forces.

At last they were released to go.

"I'm going to suggest that we go back to Appleby for a day or two," was the surprising next remark of Edward.

"Why should we want to do that?" said the still shell-shocked Rhoda.

"Because I have a suspicion that the answer to this lies there, not here on this side of the Pennines."

Rhoda reluctantly agreed providing they could stay in the same hotel. A phone call later they were booked in.

It was with heavy hearts that they reversed their journey. Edward particularly so because he had realised that both he and Rhoda might be thought to be implicated in a conspiracy. He didn't share that thought with Rhoda, though he would love to have been able to do so, rather than bear it himself in addition to their overburdening loss. A measure of their utter torment was that they didn't even notice that they were again driving past the lane down to Waters Meet.

As Rhoda drove to try to get some distraction, in his lawyer's way Edward tried to review all the events of the past few days. He tried to picture all the personalities they had met and to weigh them in the scales of justice, so to speak. Try as he would, he simply could not identify even the slightest concern which might help the police enquiry.

For her part, Rhoda's thoughts were more relating to Edward's frame of mind consequent on such a hugely disappointing outcome at the end of his chase.

All Edward could console himself with was the undoubted fact that a unique work of art could not appear on the sales circuit without instant recognition. If only the police could move fast enough to prevent it disappearing into a vault somewhere, perhaps not to emerge for decades.

"I just can't believe that after such a fruitful search all seems to have gone belly-up in such a dramatic way," moaned a distraught Rhoda.

In her moment of acute distress she allowed herself an expression normally alien to her and not often heard in her circle in Berkhamsted.

For a while Edward remained silent, his only immediate way to deal with intense sadness.

After a while they both began to rationalise the situation as best they could.

Edward spoke first.

"Look, dear. Not so long ago we had no inkling of the existence of this painting, let alone that we would see it and hold it in our hands."

Rhoda got the gist of his thinking and chipped in...

"If it still exists and doesn't end up for years in the safe of a private collector in Hong Kong or somewhere there must be a chance that we will see it again."

"Let's face it, Rhoda" added Edward, "it never was ours and really never could be if we are honest with ourselves. Let's hope that whoever has got it will make a mistake that brings it back undamaged to the attention of the art world."

"Yes," said Rhoda, "the thief must have realised it is something special."

With these thoughts they felt a little, but only a little comforted. In fact, they realised that it wasn't just sharing the adventure of finding the painting that had brought them closer together but coping with the disaster which had befallen them as a result. They knew it was a material loss, not a life-changing event, nevertheless it was a severe jolt to the happy retirement period they were now entering. A hug and a kiss helped them to move on to the difficult task of being involved in a serious mystery, probably a serious crime.

PART 6

When a man's loss comes to him from his gain
Robert Browning

CHAPTER 25

Friday 2nd August

The following morning at Penrith headquarters Detective Chief Inspector Jean Greenhalgh of Cumbria CID was working through details of yesterday's messages from Ripon. She didn't relish inter-county business which invariably resulted in much extra paperwork. She had assigned Detective Inspector Nigel Peel and Detective Sergeant Annabel Mansfield to the case of theft so that they could make a few checks of the story given to colleagues at Ripon by the Dendrons. She didn't expect it to occupy too much of their valuable time. The main responsibility surely had to lie with Ripon. Anyway it was only about a painting. Why should Ripon bother with that?

The day dragged on with yet more paperwork interrupting, she always thought, the real business of detection. It also kept her from her hobby of pottery, which helped mitigate stress. Thumping a lump of clay was an ideal way of coping with the stress of work. For her, she thought, the delicate and sensual moulding on her wheel was a parallel for her management of her team. Did she know her nickname (in the nick!) was 'Potter', because they sometimes felt more like malleable objects being fed into her kiln? Of course she knew. It was her business to know everything. In reality her view of the team was somewhere in between the extremes and they had great respect for her as a good cop who got results once she put her hand to the wheel, so to speak.

***

Just after lunch came an insistent telephone call from uniform division which left her rapidly putting on one side a mere theft.

A report had come in from a hiker on the Pennine Way above Dufton who had come across a quad bike on its side on the track near to the edge of High Cup Nick with no apparent owner. Being curious he had peered over the edge of the path and thought he could see something below on the scree at the base of the cliff. Horrified that the bike owner might have been thrown off to his destruction below, and quite unable to get down there even if it had looked that anything might be done, he had phoned 999.

***

The mountain rescue team was mobilised and joined by a constable who had some experience of these mountains as a keen walker himself. Because he had to work with them he was given permission to go in mountain boots and an anorak over his uniform. Their Land Rover could get about two miles up the track from Dufton, but after that it was necessary to walk. The volunteer rescue team were no strangers to tragedy in the mountains. In some ways they felt more needed and more respected when the call was like this one rather than to shepherd an inexperienced walker with no navigation skills.

Together they accessed as quickly as possible what sadly turned out to be the body of a young man who appeared to have fallen nearly a hundred feet onto rock near to the pinnacle on which the cobbler was supposed to have repaired shoes. A paramedic in the team was certain that nothing could be done for the victim and the team was about to recover the body when PC Hodgson called a halt. It had occurred to him that the simple explanation of a tumble from the quad bike might be just that – too simple. A quad bike up here was highly likely to belong to a farmer inspecting his sheep and such an experienced person would not be likely to take such a tumble.

He asked for no disturbance of the bike or the body by the rescue team and made a call for reinforcements including a detective and forensic pathologist as well as a recovery team. Then he set about interviewing the walker and preventing any disturbance of the ground around the bike and the edge of the cliff.

Reinforcements in the form of DCI Greenhalgh and Dr Ian Pentridge duly arrived by helicopter. Immediately she took charge but not before congratulating PC Hodgson on his judgement. She was never a person to allow her rank to belittle juniors.

"What do you make of it, Constable? Why did alarm bells ring?"

"Yes ma'am. Two things bothered me. I thought that he might be a farmer and therefore have skills on a quad bike even on mountain sides. Also I reckoned that the upturned bike wasn't near enough to the edge to have thrown him over the cliff and didn't look to be on ground which would have turned it over."

"Do you reckon he's right, Pentridge?"

"Well quad bikes aren't quite my thing, but I feel he could well be right."

"What about the overturning?"

"Two things," said Pentridge. "Although the ground is hard just here there are some signs of tyre tracks which show where the bike was standing as it tipped. I think it flipped without any forward movement. There isn't any reason why it should have done and even if it did, he would have had a pretty good chance of saving himself before going over the edge."

"Could he simply have suicidally jumped over the cliff?"

"If he did, why would the bike have been on its side?"

"Are you thinking it was deliberately turned over to give the impression of accident?" ventured the chief inspector. It was beginning to dawn on her that distinguishing between a genuine mountain accident and a crime might not be easy. Unfortunately adventurers in the hills did sometimes meet with disaster or a worker needing to drive a quad, perhaps to rescue a sheep or something, might occasionally come to grief.

"Here's a measuring tape, Constable. Measure every aspect of this area and make a little sketch and photographs before anything is moved. Can they move the body, Pentridge?"

"Yes if they handle it so as to cause no further lesions and bring it carefully up the scree to the west side of the Nick. Get the constable to go down and mark where the body is."

"Yes sir, Yes ma'am," said Hodgson immediately.

It took time for the formalities and the difficult task of recovery. Ascending the Nick from the valley below is at best a scramble, and with an inert load, a slow task even for a mountain rescue team. But it wasn't safe to get the chopper any closer to the cliff side and difficult to land it near enough in the valley.

If it hadn't been for the tragic circumstances the young constable would have been revelling in this adventure. Perhaps he might even get a ride in the helicopter. But he didn't. To begin with he was pretty certain that he knew the identity of the body. In any case there wasn't room for him as well as the body bag. Then DCI Greenhalgh ordered him to stay with the bike until she could get it checked out by SOCOs. That meant several hours of guarding it but at least that kept him out of the office for another few hours and he was quite happy up here in the hills.

As she boarded the 'copter, DCI Greenhalgh had a call telling her that there was a report of a missing person; a young farmer named Jason Cartright from Dufton who hadn't returned home the previous night from what his family assumed was an overindulgence in Appleby.

CHAPTER 26

If it was a long day for Detective Chief Inspector Greenhalgh, it was an even longer one for Constable Hodgson. He laboured at his report because he sensed that it was going to be important and may have a crucial bearing on the case. Would it be forgotten that he was the one who had trekked up to the Nick and back, as well as helping the detective team?

Well it wouldn't. After being given the go-ahead by her superintendent, DCI Greenhalgh had been on the phone to her counterpart in the uniform division to plead that Hodgson should be seconded for a few days to help with the enquiry. She readily admitted that she had had little to do with the case so far except ask the right questions whilst Hodgson and Pentridge had supplied highly relevant answers. She viewed the constable as a very bright young man who would go far in his chosen career. It was agreed. The Super had also agreed that there might be suspicious circumstances here.

All leave was cancelled for the team including the weekend.

***

Next day Greenhalgh assembled her team for a briefing on the death.

Detective Inspector Peel and Sergeant Mansfield were, for the moment, withdrawn from the stolen painting enquiry in the interest of urgent priority. With a name like Peel, it was not surprising that he was known in the team as 'Clapper' though there were some who would have sneaked in 'Clanger' if they thought he wasn't listening.

She began the procedures with a statement that Pentridge had recovered a driving licence in the name of Jason Cartright from a wallet in the left-hand pocket of the anorak, and his mobile phone.

PC Hodgson was asked to recount his experiences at High Cup Nick on the previous day, Friday and to add his interpretation of what might have happened the evening before in this fairly remote spot. Not used to presenting a case, Hodgson at first was hesitant especially until encouraged by his new and temporary boss. After reading to them his report of the facts, he ventured to add extra thoughts.

"Dufton is part of my beat," he said. "I know (hastily corrected to knew) Jason Cartright and consider him to have been a skilled upland farmer, absolutely at home on a quad bike on rough ground. I can't believe that he upturned the bike and fell over the cliff, even if he was taken ill. The measurements of tyre marks, distance from the edge, position of the bike all argue against it. There were no obvious signs of a struggle or of slip marks on the grassy edge of the cliff."

"Thanks Constable," added the Detective Chief Inspector. "I consider that report to give us reason to suspect foul play. Any arguments against that from the rest of you?"

"Well, I won't disagree," came from the DI (who wasn't at all happy at the prominence being given to a uniform branch constable's views). "But it doesn't get us much further if we are to prove it. What else do we have to go on?"

DS Mansfield chipped in here to ask if there was a report

177

from the pathologist yet.

Greenhalgh took a file from her desk and summarised Pentridge's notes:

Firstly he underlined Hodgson's comments at the scene and agreed with the interpretation of the measurements made there.

The compound injuries to the body he said, were consistent with a fall from a great height onto sharp rocks, some of them likely to have been fatal even if sustained alone. The position of the body indicated that the fall commenced at the edge of the cliff near to the quad bike. The cliff was so steep, almost vertical, that the fall was probably free until the base rocks were hit. The lesions had embedded fragments of the rock.

At this point Inspector Peel interrupted to ask if the information so far contained any real evidence of what might have caused the fall?

Chief Inspector Greenhalgh took her time to add Pentridge's last, and perhaps most significant point.

"Most of the severe trauma was around the head, the shoulders and arms, and the body lay face down. On the skin of the upper back were pressure bruises, inflicted before death, consistent with a severe push from behind, sufficient to overbalance even a strong, healthy man as Jason Cartright was. There were no other indications. Death occurred at least twelve hours before the body was discovered, that is late on Thursday evening."

This tallied with the report of Cartright's failure to return home.

There was silence in the room until broken by DCI Greenhalgh.

178

"I believe we have to conclude that we are dealing with a case of homicide by person or persons unknown."

Even the case-hardened senior investigators drew sharp breath and the juniors could not recall a more deeply disturbing experience as it involved a local man, personally known to PC Hodgson.

"I wouldn't usually be the officer to see the family of the deceased at this stage, but when I have viewed the cadaver with Pentridge and discussed our conclusions with the Super, I shall go to talk to them and go with them when the body is prepared for ID. Meanwhile, DS Mansfield, I'm giving you the deeply unpleasant task of breaking the news to them at their home. I know you will do this with the utmost care and consideration. Then organise a search of messages on Cartright's phone as soon as you are free.

"So far we have no idea whatsoever as to why this man met his death at another's hand and in such an isolated spot.

"Why was he there?"

"Did he get into an argument there which ended in him losing his life? If so, did he know his assailant and vice versa, or was it a chance encounter?

"DI Peel, set up an incident room and get your team onto a computer search of Jason Cartright. Look for any form he may have had, any record of violence by him or against him, any known family feuds or any dubious schemes connected with his business on the farm or in other ways.

"PC Hodgson, go round Dufton village discreetly and listen for any gossip, recent conversations of Cartright, perhaps in the pub. Any mentions of High Cup Nick of any kind."

"Ma'am," responded DI Peel, "whilst those enquiries get under way, may I briefly return to talk to the couple whose painting was stolen?"

"No. We must put all our resources into the Cartright case."

"With respect, ma'am, DS Mansfield contacted a PC in our Appleby nick yesterday and found that the owners of the painting had returned to their hotel there instead of continuing their journey home to Hertfordshire. Moreover the painting was of a local scene. In fact the scene of the death. Now why would they do that? It's a long shot, but the painting could have been valuable. Do you think the theft and the tragedy could be connected, and we should interview them?"

"It certainly is a long shot, Peel, but we are clutching at straws and we need a lead somewhere. It's half an hour to Appleby, let's say an hour to talk to them and half an hour back. Don't make it any more and get back here, pronto.

"Take Mansfield when she is back."

"Yes ma'am. Will do."

***

Peel had secretly become interested in the painting theft. The Ripon colleagues had told him that the owners had described it as a Turner watercolour. This hadn't meant much to the officers and didn't seem to be of much importance. However, the owners were known to have spent the last few days in Appleby and to have visited Dufton on a hike. There was just enough there to arouse Peel's curiosity. Jean Greenhalgh cultivated curiosity in her staff. It was the quality she most admired in a detective.

On the journey to Appleby Annabel was intrigued as Peel

used her as an audience to rehearse his new-found bits of googled information about this man Turner. He didn't leave prominent stones unturned when preparing to interview and figured rightly that the Dendrons would be more forthcoming to someone who could engage in some conversation on their home ground.

CHAPTER 27

Jean Greenhalgh soon considered that if this was an opportunistic killing, the chances of finding a killer operating at such a remote spot would be slim unless a hiker or perhaps farmer came forward having witnessed something. She needed to put out a public call for information. Always reluctant to take this step, she consulted her superintendent.

If Greenhalgh was right and this was not a planned killing, it became essential to establish a motive quickly if a culprit was to be found. As yet, she could see no reason why such an apparently decent man should meet such a terrible end.

***

With all weekend arrangements cancelled, the team assembled to report the day's work and thrash out ideas. It was Greenhalgh's approach to get everyone involved and free to chip in. She started by announcing that PC Hodges had been temporarily given the rank of detective constable.

Then easy bits first.

"As usual we need to invent a code name for the killer. Any ideas?"

Subdued mutterings were heard then Peel suggested 'Mallard'.

"Mallard did you say?" queried the boss.

"Yes Mallard. For two reasons. One of the painter

Turner's first names was Mallord. Goodness knows why. In addition Mallard is the name of the first steam locomotive to reach 100 mph and it might encourage us to work with utmost speed on this enquiry."

The others sniggered a little because they always considered Clapper to be a bit of an intellectual manqué, though they had to admit that this name had a certain ring to it. It had the advantage that it might refer to duck or drake. They all agreed on it especially Annabel who liked birdwatching in her time off.

***

A significant start.

Now the DCI got underway. She called on DI Peel and DS Mansfield.

"What did you make of the Dendrons?"

"They seemed straight enough," said Peel immediately. "Cagey though about the painting."

"Wouldn't you be?" reckoned DS Mansfield. "From what you were saying in the car, it's likely to be worth a bob or two."

"Well I think it is," rejoined Clapper. "It's anybody's guess until actually sold, but I wouldn't be surprised if it turned out to be at least a quarter of a million if genuine and unknown and of a new scene. We're talking 200 years old and by a master of his art. Perhaps no better known English artist of his time except maybe Constable (a rather appropriate name in the circumstances, he added rather drily). I've searched Wikipedia and that seems the general view. We did press them to explain their moves over the last few days, and describe people they may have come into contact with. The main ones turned out to be in Dufton at the Stag, at Appleby Castle would you believe, ma'am, and in Kendal."

DS Mansfield produced a list of names, places and connections.

It was the Dufton ones which DCI Greenhalgh seized on because DC Hodgson was still there, interviewing as many villagers as he could, most of whom he knew. 'Hodge', as he had rapidly become known to the team, was immediately called by Greenhalgh.

"Talk to Simon whatever he's called, Cartright's friend. Ask for any information on the southern couple (they're called Dendron). If you know someone called 'old Ernest' pump him too. Try the barman. See if you can find a couple from Leeds staying at the nearby caravan park. Listen to what anyone overheard, however trivial it seems. Then get back to me as soon as you can."

Her next questions were in a slightly different voice. Could it be that she was just a little overawed by mention of Appleby Castle? Is this dodgy ground in the county? She thought her superintendent may think so, or at least the chief constable might. But she was determined to pursue it. The days of that kind of deference should have gone. Satisfied by Peel and Mansfield that this could be fruitful ground she announced her intention to do that part of the enquiry herself with Mansfield's help.

Her juniors almost succeeded in suppressing giggles at the thought of the enquiry reaching local 'aristocracy' and Potter being ever so slightly obsequious.

"It's looking as if your hunch about the painting's involvement needs some more follow-up, Inspector," she conceded. "At the very least, the Dendrons come into the frame through their admitted Dufton connection. No pun intended," she hastily added.

"I called at the garage in Appleby, ma'am," added DS Mansfield.

"They supplied and serviced Jason Cartright's quad bike. It was in good condition and not at all likely to turn over unless very badly driven. Cartright was a skilled rider."

"Good work, Sergeant. I feel your joint work in Appleby is beginning to open the shutters a bit."

She was interrupted by a call from Hodgson.

"Can I have more time, here?" he pleaded. "I think people are talking and the Dufton end is opening up a bit."

"You certainly may, and I'll send Inspector Peel out to help."

"Inspector, join Hodgson and get as much as you can together. Remember it's his patch and people are far more likely to open up to him."

"Wait here Mansfield, I'll be back in a moment."

That's what it took to get the Super's agreement for a visit to the castle and a call made by the boss to make an appointment. Then down to the yard, sign for a car and off to Appleby.

There always had to be a sense of urgency in such cases, but the more the painting intruded, the more Greenhalgh felt a different kind of pressure. If it had played a part, and was so valuable, it might all too quickly disappear as evidence, maybe even out of the country. All her initial dismissal of its relevance was gone.

On the way, there was a call from Hodgson to the effect that Cartright's favourite pub in Appleby was near the castle and they should perhaps call in to see if anything could be picked up there. It was agreed that DS Mansfield should be dropped there, but be admitted to the castle later to join her boss if anything relevant emerged.

**

Caroline received DCI Greenhalgh with great courtesy. When it was explained that her mission might be connected with the painting, but had arisen because of a grisly murder in the hills above Dufton, she quickly offered as much help as she could. DS Mansfield would be welcome to join them as soon as she was free.

Firstly she asserted that she knew the Dendrons and that they had been in touch yesterday with their dreadful news of the loss of the painting. Anything she could do or say to help with that, she would. But she had no knowledge of the gruesome events described. News of that had not yet reached the castle which to some extent was designed to separate itself and its inhabitants from the world outside.

Her story of the Dendrons' visits to the castle, her new friendship with them and the search for the painting matched exactly with the Dufton stories, which had been extracted separately from the pair by Peel and Mansfield and themselves tallied. It seemed unlikely that such detail could have been the product of a conspiracy between the three. If it was, it would take a bit of breaking. But no matter. That is what policing is all about.

DS Mansfield was, if anything, less overawed by admission to the inner sanctums of the castle than was her boss. Perhaps it was a generation thing where deference has become less obstructive in the young than it used to be. When settled she added a significant fact to the enquiry, gleaned at the pub down the road. A young man from the castle, known to the landlord as George had met Jason Cartright there five nights ago. He remembered the occasion because it was the first night of his duty at the bar that week. No, he didn't overhear their conversation mainly because it was uncharacteristically quiet and short. Both had left long before closing time.

Caroline blanched at hearing this.

"I do have a young man called George who works here. He is a good worker and helps with all sorts of odd jobs. He was around when the Dendrons were here and helped the search a little bit by going down into town to get a locksmith. But I don't think he was there at any other time as far as I can remember. You should talk to him. I've always considered him to be a fine young man, anxious to help if perhaps ever so slightly gullible. I will send for him when you are ready."

Caroline had a very easy way with her employees and soon helped George to relax a little after his initial shocked reaction to meeting the police pair.

DCI Greenhalgh asked Caroline if they could withdraw a little whilst the young DC Mansfield interviewed the boy alone. It gave the Chief a chance to assess Caroline's reliability as a potential witness, whilst making, she hoped, the interview of George somewhat less intimidating for him.

"Hello George," began the plain-clothes junior, "My name is Annabel Mansfield. You can call me Annabel. Do you have another name?"

"Yes," said George, I'm called George Slater 'cos my dad and 'is before 'im were roofers. Boys at school used to say I weren't quite right int' rafters. But I am. I knows my way round all sorts o' stuff."

"Did you have a friend called Jason?" probed the sergeant.

"I did, but I've 'erd he copped it on 'is quad up at t'Nick. I'm sad 'cos he liked me and axed me for little jobs."

"What sort of jobs, George?" she asked.

At this he became visibly upset.

"Will I be in real trouble?" he asked anxiously.

"Not bad trouble," he was told, "if you help me with my questions."

Bit by bit the story of the tin box and the £20 paid came out.

"Did Jason tell you why he wanted the box?"

"Well 'e said as 'ow he were after some old papers from t' castle, a sort of old treasure hunt. There were another box found later by Miss Caroline and 'er friends. 'Cos I were sent to town to fetch Walter to bust it open. They found summat important in t' wooden box, but Jason found nought in 'is.

"And I see'd 'er two days gon' puttin' a package in t' back 'o friends' car for goin' off t' Yorkshire. I rang Jason to tell 'm might be t' treasure. I's got a mobile tha knows," he said proudly.

That was about the end of his testimony, but very much the beginning of Annabel's sharp realisation that this could be the breakthrough they needed. She signalled to her boss that they needed to talk quickly, perhaps not in front of Caroline. But within minutes Caroline confirmed the parts of George's story which had involved her, including the departure of the Dendrons' car with the precious painting in the boot. A minor complication was the appearance in the story of the locksmith who may have discovered what was in the box by listening in. Another one to check out, though he didn't seem very likely to be involved.

CDI Greenhalgh pressed Caroline for more detail of the painting which she agreed to give only if the Dendrons were prepared to tell what they knew. When they could be brought together though interviewed separately, it took very little time to convince all three that more knowledge of the painting was crucial to the police enquiry. Very reluctantly they revealed that it was a potentially very valuable painting of High Cup Nick. They explained that only the three of them plus the expert in Kendal were party to that discovery.

But it linked the painting clearly to the site of Jason's death!

CHAPTER 28

Next day at the incident room, Jean Greenhalgh asked DS Mansfield to tell the assembled team what George and the painting's owners had disclosed.

It was immediately obvious to them all that Jason had at the very least been involved in the theft of the painting. Could that explain why he was at High Cup Nick?

DI Peel suggested that on examination of the painting, Cartright would have been bound to recognise the site of the viewpoint.

DC Hodgson, however, expressed the view that because Jason did know it so well, there would be no need to go there to check. Unless, he surmised, someone else was involved who didn't know the location and needed to be convinced by Jason that it mattered. So someone else who wasn't from Dufton but with a particular knowledge of Turner and his paintings in the area. Could this be the murderer?

DI Peel was the only one of them with any feel for the work of Turner. He chipped in the offering that it probably had to be a dealer or expert in fine art, most probably of Turner's travels in the North.

DCI Greenhalgh reminded everyone of the fourth person with knowledge of the painting's existence, namely the expert in Kendal. If he had been told of the theft, could he have tried to retrieve the painting, with or without the knowledge of Caroline or the Dendrons? A quick call to Appleby established that the Dendrons and Caroline claimed that he had not been told of the theft. That would have to be checked by his testimony so DI Peel was despatched to Kendal to get that side of the story.

Meanwhile two steps were set in motion at headquarters in Penrith. Firstly they were asked to again check Cartright's phone found on his body to confirm or otherwise George's account of his interactions with Jason in addition to see if any other recorded messages might have a bearing on the case. Secondly they were asked to come up with a list of all art dealers in the region and to check any special interest in paintings originating from Turner's northern travels.

***

The phone yielded its secrets much more quickly than the second search.

Jason didn't use his phone often and it wasn't sophisticated enough for social media. DC Hodgson contributed his opinion that Jason wouldn't have been into social media in any case. His socialising was far more likely to have been face to face in the Stag at Dufton.

Calls to and from George were quickly located and they vindicated the latter's evidence given to Annabel. Otherwise the analysts at headquarters could find only two or three calls to a number near Carlisle. One of these was to arrange a meeting near Penrith with a third party on the morning after the one with George at the pub in Appleby. It concerned a tin box, just as George had described. but added the need to break it open because it was thought to contain a valuable unnamed painting.

At this point, DC Hodgson consulted his notes and added that Simon had told him of a conversation with Jason at the Stag, after they had overheard talk between the Dendrons and visitors from Leeds, and with old Ernest. All had been asked about Turner and a possible visit by him to Dufton. Ernest had been overheard confirming a visit, and the possibility of a painting in a box at the castle. He didn't think they had heard that the box was wooden.

Moreover, Jason had described a link between himself and an art dealer, and had talked about a possible dodgy deal. Simon insisted that he had distanced himself completely from this scheme. He was devastated by Jason's death.

The team considered that it was inconceivable that Ernest could have had any involvement in Jason's death and pretty unlikely that the Leeds couple had because DC Hodgson. had established that they had apparently left for home before it occurred.

Another call from headquarters described a text from Jason to the mobile number on which the meeting near Penrith had been arranged.

This time it was more enigmatic. It read, 'Got WC. Poss HCN. CU HW 8 TNT.'

First reactions of the team were to pick out HCN (Hydrogen cyanide), CU (copper) and TNT (explosive) as if it was a terrorist message. Was something dangerous hidden in a Water Closet?

But DS Mansfield was thoughtful. She had found an interest in coded information ever since a holiday visit to the Bletchley code-breaking centre. She also liked doing crosswords, especially cryptic ones.

After only a few moments she ventured:

"Got water colour. Possibly High Cup Nick. See you 8.00 tonight. I can't get the reference to HW though."

But 'Hodge' could. He knew a spot on the Pennine Way known as Hannah's Well. With some enthusiasm he pointed out that this is near where the quad bike was found.

"That would be a definite invitation to meet Jason on the way to where he died. Why would they go to all the trouble of meeting up near the Nick?", questioned Annabel.

Meanwhile DI Peel, now back from Kendal, agreed with her reading of the message and added,

"The painting would be a watercolour. That is the medium Turner used to bring to life his sketches of his journeys. If the unknown person didn't know the terrain, it is conceivable that they would agree to go up the track to see and compare the painting with the scene. If a meeting took place, could two people ride a quad bike on the Pennine Way track?"

DC Hodgson was sure they could. He had often seen farmers giving lifts, not just to their dogs, when off road, though it would be illegal on the highway and possibly on a registered agricultural vehicle.

"It would be easier to overlook, though, he admitted as the local PC. In any case he said, we are dealing with a crime here when rules don't apply."

"What about being seen by hikers on their way down?" pressed Peel.

"I don't think it would be a big risk at that time of night," thought Hodgson. "Most walkers would have reached Dufton by then, and if not, might have been mildly interested, but not alarmed to see a rider going tandem. No one seems to have reported anything unusual."

"How long would it take to ride up to where we found the

quad?" asked DCI Greenhalgh.

"The first two miles are easy track which a quad should do in half an hour," said Hodge. "The last mile slower, but no more than one hour in total."

DCI Greenhalgh called for stiff coffees all round, then began her summary of a likely scenario:

"Jason gets a message from George that a package is in Dendron's car and they are travelling East probably across to the A1 (M).

"Jason drives fast and spots them before Scotch Corner. He parks near them and waits his opportunity to steal the package.

"Back in Dufton he unpacks it and recognises what he thinks could be a watercolour of High Cup Nick.

"He sends the cryptic message to an unknown person to meet him that night.

"Presumably Jason is hoping to do a lucrative deal. That might suggest an art dealer, as mentioned by Simon.

"Could it be that the unknown person entices Jason to ride to High Cup Nick, shoves him over the cliff, upends the bike and sets off down with the painting? By now it will be about eight thirty allowing the murderer to walk briskly back to Dufton to enter the village under the cover of dusk with the painting in a backpack. DC Hodgson thinks it would take a bit over an hour from Hannah's Well.

"His or her car parked for three or four hours in the evening wouldn't attract any attention.

"The quad bike is found next morning and the incident reported.

"We need to review every suspect in the light of this timetable," concluded the DCI. "Get the link with Carlisle traced, Mansfield, and have the caller interviewed by the Carlisle force asap."

Annabel went off to do as she was bidden.

"We need to review every suspect in the light of this timetable," added the DCI. "As a young, healthy guy, Simon could presumably fit this scheme. Get up to Dufton, Hodge and check him out for alibi."

***

The Carlisle caller did indeed turn out to be an art dealer, but at the age of seventy-one he was not deemed likely to fit the bill by the Carlisle force, but might have to be re-visited.

Simon had been at the Stag with friends for part, but not all of the evening, a fact supported by the landlord. A few more interviews of local lads would deal with that, and a more searching interview with Simon. He did admit that he knew that Jason thought there was a potentially valuable painting, but that he was completely shocked to hear of Jason's death.

CHAPTER 29

The DCI spent lunch chewing on a sandwich sent up with coffee and chewing over her view of the case thus far.

The juniors were bouncing ideas around during a hasty lunch in the canteen before DCI Jean would join them again. She encouraged this. Very often the best insight came in informal moments outside her office when the younger officers were briefly relieved of the responsibility which she could never put aside.

A rather diffident DC Hodgson (he still hadn't come to terms properly with his new status, though he did have confidence that he could contribute to the investigation) asked timorously how they viewed his new boss. He had never been part of a team led by a woman.

Clapper was quick to dispel any concern the DC may have had. After his original wariness he was keen to make Hodge feel relaxed. Before answering his question he invited the new man to call him 'Clapper' – an appellation he secretly liked, and DS Mansfield by her first name, at least in these relaxed surroundings. "But for God's sake don't call the DCI 'Potter' in her hearing." They took it for granted he didn't mind 'Hodge'.

"She is a first class detective and a great person to work with once you have got used to her style. She doesn't come over all 'boss' and does respect our contributions. Indeed she lets us feel that we are leading the enquiry, though we know fine well that she is gently, shrewdly weighing up everything and quietly asking all the right questions. But there is real discipline underneath. You are lucky, Hodge to have joined this team."

Encouraged, Hodge said "What do you reckon to, er, Potter's theory so far, does it fit how Cartright might have behaved?"

"Well she always tries to get inside the heads of both victim and any supposed killer. One of her strengths is understanding behaviour patterns," replied Annabel. "From your local knowledge do you think her reconstruction of the scene makes sense?"

Hodgson was much better on the practicalities, and here was a query which he was qualified to argue.

"Jason was last seen in the village about seven forty-five. As a hill farmer, he would have readily jumped on his quad bike to get quickly onto the fell above his in-by land. The High Cup track is pretty good for about two and a half miles from the village. Then it starts to get rough and a bit bouldery for the few hundred yards before we found the quad. Not even Jason could have ridden it much further up. I guess he could make it to there in about half an hour from Dufton. After that it would be a few minutes walking to a view of the Nick. Some of his sheep would normally graze there on the few good patches near the top. Swaledales are used to mountain foraging."

"How long would it take to walk back down to the village from there?" mused Annabel.

"Well he didn't walk back, poor blighter," said Hodge.

"No, tragically he didn't," chipped in Annabel, "but his killer did."

"A good hill walker could do it fairly easily in an hour without arousing too much curiosity in any potential witness. It's all downhill."

"That gives us some kind of timetable," said Annabel. "We need to check movements of all possible suspects from about teatime to late on Thursday."

CHAPTER 30

They didn't mind when called back urgently by the DCI now that they had sorted things a bit in their own minds.

"Now tell me what your thoughts have been over lunch." Potter began. She always encouraged them to share their thinking and especially liked the putative timetable.

"Put it up on the whiteboard," she said to Annabel who happily complied whilst Hodge helped by filling in a few more details from his personal experience of hiking up and down the track to the Nick. Known moves and locations of all suspects were added to the timetable.

She filled them in on DI Peel's report that the Abbot Hall expert (who turned out to be called Frank Manson) could be completely ruled out. He had been at a meeting all day on a fundraising venture for the museum and gallery. He could hardly have a stronger alibi than the recorded fact that the meeting had clinched a £50,000 grant to support the ever increasing significance of the collection as being of national status.

It also ruled out Caroline who as a trustee of the gallery was involved in celebrating the grant by sharing one of her laid-down champagne bottles with the other trustees. To her it was also a way of putting aside worrying thoughts of a combined loss of the Turner and an apparently associated death.

Now Jean set DI Peel onto the next task. When he had

quickly taken in what was on the board, he added a column to enter notes of known facts about each. Standard procedure, no doubt, but particularly helpful when the schedule of movements was so critical to understanding the opportunities of each suspect.

The senior officer asked Peel to add the names of all possible players regardless of the team's suspicions of them at this stage.

First came the Dendrons, man and wife separately. For a moment DC Hodgson protested on the grounds that he could see no reason why the owners of the painting should have stolen it, let alone killed someone to do so.

'Potter' immediately intervened on the correct grounds that no assumptions must be inserted at this stage. He nodded and recognised being on a pretty steep learning curve.

Next on Peel's list were Caroline and the Abbot Hall curator marked up as Frank Manson. Even though 'Clapper' had apparently found them eliminated, he wasn't completely prepared to take that step formally until alibis had been thoroughly checked by colleagues in Kendal.

The two following names were George at the castle and Simon from Dufton.

Simon knew that the painting might be very valuable, and was in regular contact with the victim, probably knew his moves accurately, and had very good local knowledge.

Next was the mysterious 'dealer' from Carlisle.

At this point DC Hodgson stood up to attract notice.

"Go ahead," said Jean. "We need everyone keeping each other on the ball."

"I think," he said, "we should still keep the Leeds pair on the board. I know we think they had probably left Dufton and gone home, but that should be checked again?"

"Quite right," his superior agreed. "Is there anyone else we mustn't miss?"

No one else had entered the discussion so far, but they were all aware that if the next few hours didn't come up tricks they were literally back to the drawing board with new names to find. At this stage they were all reluctant to countenance the unspoken possibility that linking the theft with the murder could be a serious error leading them to bark completely up the wrong tree. The thought caused Annabel to dream up the highly irrelevant question of whether this cliché was to a dog barking when visiting a tree, or merely the covering protecting the tree. She surprised herself that in such a serious situation her mind could wander so trivially.

Meanwhile Jean Cartright was carefully examining the schedule set out before her.

"It seems to me", she concluded "that the critical time from seven forty-five p.m. to ten or so is correct and that anyone shown not to be able to be at the scene during those hours must be eliminated from our enquiry."

"There's something about this that I don't like, ma'am," piped up Hodgson.

"The victim is known to have left Dufton at about seven forty-five, not to return, but unless Mallard stayed up on the fell overnight, he must have been back in Dufton by dark or at any rate used a head torch to get down. Sunset was eight thirty that night and it was pretty dark by nine thirty. Jason was on his quad bike and could have reached the point where he died by eight thirty as planned, leaving his killer to do the deed and get back to Dufton with no more than one hour to spare, or at the very most an hour and a half."

"That sounds OK doesn't it?" added Peel. "What's the problem?"

"I can't see how any of our suspects could possibly have got up to the Nick at the required time, done the deed and got back down again to fit our matrix. All of them have alibis for at least part of that period."

This caused them all to sit and stare at the whiteboard going over the entries for each suspect with a tooth comb. They were all aware that many of their suspects were being crossed out on the board.

"We'll have a short break whilst we all think deeply about this," said Potter. "Is there something we are all missing in what we've got so far, or is there a big gap in our info?"

***

Indeed there was. It was filled by a call on the DCI's phone a few minutes later.

An off-road bicycle had been found in a ditch near to where the track down from the Nick joined the road into the centre of Dufton; a distance of only about 200 metres.

"Do you know a chap called Thomas in Dufton who runs a bike hire business, Hodgson? Is he reliable?"

"Yes, I do, ma'am. He hires out bikes to tourists, including off-road bikes for visitors who want to ride part of the Pennine Way. It's quite a thriving thing in the summer, and yes, he is reliable. I've known him for years."

"Well it turns out he hired a bike on Thursday to a woman who gave her name as what he thought sounded like a plant name. That's how he entered it in his records. He regrets not listening more carefully because the bike was never returned, it's only just turned up and he doesn't know who hired it. It wasn't anyone he knows locally.

"You'd better get there as quick as you can, Mansfield. Take the van and a helper. Impound the bike, wrap it in plastic and send it back here to forensics whilst you interview Thomas and get anything else he remembers. Report back asap or before."

"Is this the breakthrough we need?" breathed Clapper. "Can the timing problem be helped if we shove a bike in there somewhere?"

"What do you reckon, Hodgson as a local?"

"What I do know is that I can ride a mountain bike down that track in less than twenty minutes" It's a thing I often do off duty. Not that track always, of course, but I have done it quite a few times. It takes a bit of skill, but lots of people could do it at a fair speed."

"Who's a competent cyclist amongst the list?" thought Clapper. "That's not a question we thought of asking anyone in interviews."

Actually, he suddenly recalled:

"There is a note in yesterday's interview with Edward Dendron that one of his pastimes was hill walking and he's still quite fit, but he also mentioned in passing that Rhoda D. is more keen on cycling than on walking, but she is now doing both."

Potter quietly complimented him on his long-standing ability to absorb case paperwork quickly and remember the details.

Not to be outdone, young Hodgson threw in the reminder that Mrs Dendron's first name is Rhoda.

"You know," he firmly and proudly asserted, "Rhoda

Dendron – a plant name!"

He didn't often speak with exclamation marks, but felt this required it. Could it really be that the joint owner of the painting was involved in a killing to retrieve it and what could her motive possibly have been?

"We must go over her alibi now with a magnifying glass – shades of Sherlock," called Potter to the team. They did, and the fact was it didn't stand up to careful scrutiny. If a bike was involved, she just might have been able to do it.

"It's late now. Bring her in first thing tomorrow and confront her," said the DCI. "Not an arrest yet; helping us with our enquiries."

***

Next morning DI Peel met Mrs Dendron.

"Mrs Dendron, I'm sorry I have to ask you a few more questions to fill in a gap or two in our investigation."

"Of course, I'm happy to help in anything that will clear up this awful business."

"Do you consider yourself to be a competent cyclist, Mrs Dendron?" asked Clapper.

"Well yes I do," came the confident reply. "I learnt to cycle as a young girl in Essex and have kept it up ever since as my main way of keeping fit. I've never been as good a walker as Edward."

"Have you done any cycling whilst up here on holiday?"

"I wonder why you are asking? Something very curious has happened. I noticed a chap in Dufton who hires out trail bikes so I hired one on Thursday afternoon. I told you before, I was in Dufton trying to clear my head over this whole business but I didn't think of mentioning the bike because it didn't work out as planned. I wanted to go back to High Cup Nick because of all the fuss over the painting. Of course I didn't know then what was to happen up there that night, or when I was last interviewed on Thursday morning over the theft."

Clapper decided to let her talk on in the hope she might incriminate herself.

"I did hire the bike and my plan was to ride up to there. But I realised that I probably wasn't proficient enough on that kind of bike to make it up such a long and steep track and back again that evening. So I abandoned the idea. I was riding it towards Dufton when I saw a youngish chap on a quad bike near the farm. I always like to chat with locals when I'm on holiday and I soon recognised him as one to whom we had talked briefly in the Stag a few days ago. So I asked him if he ever rode his machine up the tracks. He told me that he often did for shepherding, but that he had been approached to meet someone up the track later that day, and he was going up on his quad later. I apologised for being cheeky, but I asked him if he would take the mountain bike on the back of his quad bike and leave it as far up the track as he could get it. My plan was to walk up later, but have the cycle to ride back down again. He agreed and I left the bike with him. That way, I could take my time going up on foot and enjoy the ride down. In the event I did neither."

Clapper realised that this could be all true, but it could equally be a partial account of how she had been able to deal with Cartright and fit into the matrix of moves required by Mallard.

"Why didn't you do it?" he requested.

"I had a call from Edward to come back to Appleby

because we had an invite to meet Caroline at the castle for tea."

DI Peel knew that this fitted with Caroline's evidence of her own moves and so, unless they were complicit, Rhoda was off the hook. But it left the crucial question of what happened to the bike. The other witness of that transaction was now dead.

Clapper phoned in his conclusions and set off back to Penrith to join the team.

As he drove he reflected on that question and wondered if a third party – *the* third party in fact had cashed in on this arrangement with Jason to escape from the scene. If so, Jason had unwittingly provided at least part of the means leading to his own demise.

***

Simon, and the mysterious link between Jason and someone from Carlisle remained to be investigated further in the context of the established timetable.

At first it seemed that the Carlisle connection would be easily dealt with. The local force tracked him down, interviewed him and rapidly established that he admitted to meeting Jason at Penrith to examine the contents of a box. It was a waste of time, he had said, because the contents were no more than some old papers.

Of course, he could still have returned to Dufton to meet Jason again, this time with the painting in Jason's possession.

Here was a strong motive of a dealer who would undoubtedly have known the value of a Turner and could possibly even have judged its likely authenticity if asked to by Jason. He was known to be rather elderly, but was there some way in which he could have been involved, much in the way as they had conjectured for Mrs Dendron? He had to be interviewed by one of the team to explore this possibility.

DS Mansfield was given this responsibility. He was asked to come to the station in Carlisle.

Annabel was able to conclude this in less than two hours.

"Did you know," she pressed, "what Cartright thought might be in the box?"

"No comment. I want a solicitor."

With one present, Annabel and a local DC, continued.

Still, "No comment."

Annabel guessed that he clearly didn't want to incriminate himself in a possible theft.

"This is not just a question of theft," she forcefully said. "We are talking about murder."

A short whisper from the duty solicitor elicited a response from the frightened man.

"Yes, I was told that there might be a Turner in the box. Yes, I would have given my right arm to get my hands on one. But I didn't go back, I didn't have any further contact with Cartright. And I didn't kill him."

"Can you account for your moves on Thursday from mid-afternoon to late evening?" challenged the sergeant.

He was very reluctant to do so.

Annabel had to admit to herself that so far they had no evidence of a second arrangement between this man and Jason. She prided herself on being a good judge of character and used to seeing when a man had something to hide, she thought.

"I say again. Where were you on the afternoon and evening on Thursday?"

"Can I have a fag?" came a whining response. The constable produced a packet kept at the station for that purpose.

"All right, I give up. But I wasn't anywhere near Cartright. I was up in Dumfries trying to buy a dodgy antiquarian book someone had nicked from Dunlanrig Castle."

"Can you prove it?" Annabel cajoled.

"Well, I reckon I got clobbered on the way back by a speed camera near Gretna and I've got eight points, so I'm bothered. And I didn't get the book, I just got booked," he said, without appreciating the irony.

Annabel left the local force to chase this one up.

***

Back at the ranch, Clapper and Hodge were interviewing Simon.

"I've never been involved in anything like this in my life," he pleaded.

"Jason was my employer, but also a good friend from school days. I've lost my best mate. I've probably lost a job as well."

"Take us through the evening of last Thursday," cajoled Clapper.

"I was at the Stag from about six for at least an hour with my mates and back at nine. They'll tell you. We had a few pints."

Clapper immediately saw a gap which was pretty much the same as their timetable required. He saw a possible breakdown in Simon's alibi at the Stag.

"Where were you between seven and nine?"

"I got a message we had a yow in trouble at t' farm. She had got her horns hooked in a fence and was a bit messed up trying to escape. It took me that time to get her sorted. Was I glad to get back to the lads."

DC Hodge interpreted 'yow' as 'ewe' for Clapper and said he would easily check that story out.

CHAPTER 31

On the one hand Jean was beginning to think that matters were becoming clearer as suspects were removed one by one from the picture. The problem was that not much was left. Her big concern was if the responsible person(s) had not featured at all in the story so far. She was happy to go back repeatedly to the whiteboard but she didn't relish going back to the drawing board.

DI Peel was speaking as she pushed such thoughts out of mind. He returned to the pair from Leeds who they thought had been discounted. For brevity they had entered these two on the board as LM for Leeds Man, and ML for Mrs Leeds.

"Well, on the board we have got the man from Leeds out on his own for most of the afternoon, but on the caravan site at seven and in the Stag from seven forty-five until ten, so that removes him from the matrix.

Mrs from Leeds, on the other hand was seen in Dufton with her husband at seven, and again at nine by other residents on the campsite. The same witness says that both were together in the Stag at nine fifteen."

"The new factor is the mountain bike," they all competed to say.

"All right, all right," were the calming words of Potter. "Could one of them have found the bike and used it to get up and down the track faster than we were calculating."

"Yes," said Hodgson. "Definitely yes. One of them

certainly could – if, and it's a very big if, he or she could have got to the scene by eight thirty, having both been seen in Dufton at seven. Both were probably fit enough to have walked up to High Cup in about one hour from then, but LM was seen again at about seven fifty by Simon coming back early from the Stag. Again, unless they are colluding, they alibi each other."

"It doesn't give Mrs Leeds [ML] an alibi though," added DS Mansfield.

"No,", agreed Greenhalgh, "but there is one other witness who was doing his garden at the roadside on the Appleby side of Dufton where the track comes down from High Cup Nick. He is prepared to swear that no one walked past him or cycled past him between seven and eight o'clock. His wife, who likes to peer round the curtain a bit in the evening, backs him up on that. After that they had gone in to watch *Strictly* on tele."

Looking at his notes, Clapper added that these local witnesses had been in agreement that they heard a quad bike nearby as they sat down to watch.

"So the timing is likely to be OK. That was probably Jason on his way up the track."

***

Yet again Constable Hodgson provided the team with a much needed lead. It was clear that his local knowledge was fundamental, but also that he had the ability to deploy it very intelligently.

"I've got the OS explorer map 19 here," he pointed out, "and you can clearly see that the path marked to High Cup Nick (HCN he came to call it) from Dufton goes over to

Teesdale about eight miles away to the east across rough ground."

DI Peel, who prided himself on having read around the case, slipped in that he knew that was the route Turner had come to sketch the Nick. Another sign of Clapper's learning.

Hodgson brought them back to the present by gathering them all round the map and sketching with his pencil another route up onto the fells from Dufton village, namely the old miners' track up to near Rundale Tarn about two miles north-west of HCN and a little higher in altitude. He explained that though this track had become very rough over the years it was easily walkable.

His punchline, however, was that in recent years, the track had been realigned in the most difficult bit, to enable 4x4's to get right onto the moor for grouse shooting. With the Glorious Twelfth being only a few days away, vehicles were often going up and down to prepare the shelter and tidy up the shooting butts on the moor. They would not have attracted particular attention. Suppose someone had driven that way?

"That's all very well, Hodge, but you said that it is still about two miles from HCN with no track between."

"That's true," conceded Hodge, "but a very fit walker could yomp across that moor."

"Could what it?" questioned Annabel.

"Could yomp it," repeated Hodge. "It's a word invented to describe the exceedingly tough crossings of moorland by the Brits during the 1982 Falklands campaign. Some of their training was up here, by the way, at Warcop so I reckon it's a suitable description."

Despite this revelation, the team looked fairly glum. Did this mean that the most likely culprit was a random walker who came across Cartright by accident and for some reason finished him off and then disappeared? The worst possible scenario of a largely random killing with no obvious motive. We haven't anyone on our whiteboard who could fit that bill, was the collective thought.

"I think we do," pronounced the DCI. "The Leeds pair are known to be very keen walkers and know this area extremely well. It's practically their second home. Many ordinary-looking vehicles these days are 4x4 and can attack some jolly bad roads. Suppose the Leeds couple have one. Caravanners often use them for towing. Get that checked. How would that fit in to our timetable?"

Clapper had a ruler out and was busy making crude measures of distances on the map.

"I make it three miles from Dufton to the top of the mine track at Rundale. A 4x4 driver used to his vehicle and knowing the track could probably do that in twenty minutes at average ten mph. Leaving Dufton at seven fifteen that would mean seven thirty-five."

More difficult was the possible way from there over the moor on foot to HCN, but with the help of Hodges they arrived at a best estimate of two miles requiring one hour or a bit less for a fit walker used to crossing heather moorland via Backstone Edge to where the quad bike was found below Hannah's Well.

"Since LM was reported in Dufton at seven fifty, that person could be his passenger Mrs Leeds, left at Rundale top. He would then scoot back down the track while she set off yomping."

A now rather excited Annabel who was glued (fortunately not literally) to the whiteboard had listed all these times. She approved of all this theorising. After adding ten minutes for the killing and twenty minutes for the mountain bike ride she came up with a time for the murderer to be back in Dufton by nine o'clock. She was convinced that Mrs Leeds could be their killer if Cartright had taken the mountain bike up on his quad and she found it, used it and then dumped it.

"Why would he take the bike up if Rhoda had pulled out of her plan to use it to cycle down as she claims?" protested Clapper.

"He wouldn't necessarily know that she had changed her mind, or because he anticipated needing to abandon the quad for the last few hundred metres and could use a cycle," prompted Hodges.

"Not being much of an outdoor type," added the DCI, "I'll have to take your words for it that all that might be a possibility. We need to arrange for a fit walker, a good off-road cyclist and a 4x4 driver to re-enact the thing for us. Then work on a motive, get any forensics we can. Meanwhile I'll put all this to the Super and see if we can bring them both in with the help of the Yorkshire force."

CHAPTER 32

At the pre-breakfast briefing the next morning DCI Greenhalgh reviewed some of the evidence needed. She explained to the team that a warrant had been issued to search the Leeds couple's caravan and especially the woman's boots and other equipment impounded. On the advice of the forensic team she had commissioned a study of material removed from the vibram soles of the boots, and from anything trapped in the Velcro of her gaiters. These articles of protective clothing beloved by all hikers in boggy conditions capture all sorts of debris and are often the last items of equipment to be meticulously cleaned. If their working hypothesis proved to be a likely scenario, evidence would be needed of Leeds female's trek across Rundale moor and along Backstone Edge.

Another team was searching the caravan for any sign of the missing painting.

***

"Results from forensic scientists have just come in," she later concluded, "and, do you know, they support our thinking."

"That could have come from anywhere in the north of England," sniffed the Super when briefed that samples of heather had been found stuck in the gaiter Velcro. She and her legal advisors were as yet unaware that a report about this heather, commissioned from experts at Durham, had included a study of the age structure of remnants of a heather-feeding insect population found in those heather samples recovered from the gaiters.

DCI Greenhalgh explained that the report cited studies made at Durham Uni twenty-five years ago, that proportions of immature forms of these insects are different in different locations, particularly different altitudes. They conceivably might be used to identify the source of the heather and work was continuing on that.

"Gosh! That sounds about as far-fetched as any evidence I've ever come across," expostulated Clapper.

"Well it might sound so," rejoined his boss, "but I'm advised that forensic entomology has been significantly developed, much of it by a Finnish scientist called Pekka Nuorteva published in the 1950s and 60s. The first time it was ever used in the UK to help to convict was probably in a trial in Lancaster eighty years ago this year. Unbelievably, similar evidence appeared in an investigation in the 1840s in Jura, that is the European area, not Scotland!"

"We don't half live and learn," muttered Clapper, but secretly he was as impressed as the rest of the team with this step forward.

"There is more to come," said the DCI. "Chemical analyses of the fragments of heather might also help to reveal the location from which they came and so might the soil adhering to the boots.

"Fragments of rock and soil from her boots agree with samples taken from the track up to Rundale, the peat on the moor and, wait for it, the track at HCN where the quad was found.

"With all this information the lab. people are willing to

testify that these samples from gaiters and boots quite likely came from Rundale moor but they cannot say exactly when."

She spelled out these conclusions one by one to emphasise what she thought was their significance.

"Our own Forensics is working on samples from the Leeds' car tyres and from the trail bike. DNA results from Cartright's clothing, the quad and the fencing stoop are also expected soon."

Potter was too professional to sound too triumphant, but she always liked to keep her team on as optimistic a plane as possible.

"Just let's hope it will stand up in court if need be," she concluded. "The Super thinks we have enough to confront and charge her and him as an accomplice. We still have a few hours left to do that before a compulsory release."

CHAPTER 33

The couple from Leeds were known only as Ash and Mavis in the Stag.

In fact at interview he confessed that he was christened Ashworth, the surname of his paternal grandfather. He was named at a time when it was not unusual to use a family name as a first.

Simon and the barman had confirmed what was known of their appearances there on the day in question and their other moves and 'spottings' had been rigorously checked.

***

The team now know that their suspects' family name was Parkinson. DCI Greenhalgh had arranged for them to be separately interviewed. Because of his local knowledge DC Hodge was to sit in on DI Peel's interview of Ashworth (may he call him Ash?) and then as an observer with the DCI and DS Mansfield, who were dealing with Mavis.

If guilty, they had clearly got a good story together which independently agreed both with each other and with witness statements. Otherwise they resorted to "no comments," perhaps on the advice of their solicitor.

They had cheekily asked for Edward Dendron that "nice legal chap they had met at the Stag" to represent them! An incredible move which was abruptly refused, of course. But it struck Jean that it was hardly an action of ordinary innocents to joke about their circumstance and suggested to Jean that it might reveal a certain criminal professionalism and confidence. But she was too professional herself to be taken in by it.

She was the confident one now on the basis of lab evidence backing the presumptions underlying all the forensic investigations. Perhaps most important of all was the linking of the suspect's DNA to samples from the back of Cartright's anorak, the bicycle handlebars and the fencing post.

***

Greenhalgh and Clapper withheld these trump cards until the two had been questioned about their movements and possible motives. The latter had become clearer as investigations by the Leeds force established that Mavis was a minor art gallery owner in the city who they had been watching for a time on suspicion of being a fence. She and her husband were known to them as Mr and Mrs Parkinson.

In a second interview The DCI sprung her obvious question.

"As an art dealer did she know of Turner?"

Yes she did. She had also heard him referred to in the bar of the Stag by that chap from the South.

"Had she overheard any conversation between Jason Cartright and Simon, his friend?"

"Well, a bit, I suppose. But the beer is good there and we were busy enjoying that and reviewing our day out."

"Did you hear any conversation between the southerners and old Ernest?"

"They were at the other end of the room and old Ernest could hardly manage more than a whisper. Anyway it was mainly in Cumbrian, not Yorkshire." Mavis denied hearing anything.

DCI Greenhalgh let all this go except for one thing.

"How do you know that the southerner is a retired lawyer?"

For the first time Mavis began to stumble. Her joke was about to rebound. She knew that to confess to having looked him up on Google would immediately reveal much more interest in the whole thing.

"Oh, someone must have mentioned it," was her lame response.

From that moment her confidence began to crack and when confronted with all the evidence, she refused to say any more, except by facial contortions.

When the officers withdrew, her solicitor advised her to go through the evidence with him and argue her case. Unless she was able to refute it, his advice was to plead guilty if charged.

Most damning of all was the DNA evidence which totally shocked her because she knew she had worn gloves throughout. Now she realised her mistakes. Yes, she had gloves for the hike across the moor, simply for warmth. But she had taken them off to handle the precious painting in order to unwrap it. In her excitement at seeing it, she had failed to put them back on before launching her attack on Jason as he stood slightly ahead of her on the edge of the precipice. It had been so easy. So had packing the painting into her small backpack. Setting up the quad bike to make it look like an accident wasn't so easy. Before handling it she had replaced her gloves. She needed a nearby abandoned fencing post to act as a lever. It had jagged edges which had torn a glove and punctured her skin – not noticed in the heat of all the action. On the bike, there was saliva on the handlebars from wiping spittle from her unaccustomed exertions.

Before being led away, she was told that she was to be arrested on charges of theft and first degree murder. She had nothing to say.

Ashworth Parkinson buckled when everything was put to him and he was arrested on conspiracy to murder. He insisted on claiming that he knew nothing of his wife's actions except for her intent to steal the painting after comparing it with the actual location in the most secretive way that they could jointly devise. Jason Cartright had been willing to go along with the plan, not knowing that it might lead to his end.

Both were charged with conspiracy to steal a valuable painting and with the murder of Jason Cartright.

CHAPTER 34

The Cumbria newspapers went to town on news of the arrests and the next day the national media led with the story. The tabloids and social media tended to emphasise such gory details as the Cumbria Police were prepared to release. The broadsheets placed more column inches on the wonderful story of the thrice lost Turner painting now that its final recovery from the Parkinsons' caravan roof lining had been announced.

***

Without displaying too much triumphalism, 'Potter' and her team rejoiced in another case closed successfully and one which they all agreed had some rather special aspects. For 'Hodge' however, there was a tinge of sadness as he prepared to return to the uniform division.

Less muted were the celebrations at Appleby Castle with the Dendrons and Frank from the Abbot Hall as Caroline's guests. As a complete surprise for them she was able to introduce them to her guest of honour, the Director of the Tate Gallery who had put everything aside to be there.

But the real centre of attention, standing on an easel out of the direct sunlight was *High Cup Nick*, by Joseph William Mallord Turner.

Everyone present agreed that they could now all rest "Appleby Ever After," whilst they toasted Turner as the greatest Landscape Painter of the North of England and the World.

THE END